JN409664

그렇습니까? 기린입니다

아시아에서는 《바이링궐 에디션 한국 대표 소설》을 기획하여 한국의 우수한 문학을 주제별로 엄선해 국내외 독자들에게 소개합니다. 이 기획은 국내외 우수한 번역가들이 참여하여 원작의 품격을 최대한 살렸습니다. 문학을 통해 아시아의 정체성과 가치를 살피는 데 주력해 온 아시아는 한국인의 삶을 넓고 깊게 이해하는 데 이 기획이 기여하기를 기대합니다.

Asia Publishers presents some of the very best modern Korean literatureto readers worldwide through its new Korean literature series <Bilingual Edition Modern Korean Literature>. We are proud and happy to offer it in the most authoritative translation by renowned translators of Korean literature. We hope that this series helps to build solid bridges between citizens of the world and Koreans through a rich in-depth understanding of Korea.

바이링궐 에디션 한국 대표 소설 034

Bi-lingual Edition Modern Korean Literature 034

Is That So? I'm A Giraffe

박민규
그렇습니까? 기린입니다

Park Min-gyu

Contents

그렇습니까? 기린입니다

Is That So? I'm A Giraffe

나의 산수

화성인들은 좋겠다. 그해 여름은 너무 무더워, 나는 늘 그런 상념에 젖고는 했다. 상고(商高)의 여름방학은 생각보다 길어서, 그런 상념에라도 빠지지 않으면 견딜 수가 없었다. 긴긴 여름, 게다가 나는 여러 일터를 전전했다. 오후엔 주유소에서, 또 밤에는 편의점에서. 있으나마나 한 여자애들이 일터마다 있긴 했지만, 있으나마나 했으므로 지루하긴 마찬가지였다. 비하자면 수성과 금성과, 있으나마나인 별들을 지나, 지구까지 오던 태양광선이 나 같은 기분이었을까? 덥지도 않고, 멀고먼,

My Arithmetic

Must be nice to be a Martian. Summer that year was so muggy, I couldn't help thinking that way. The vocational high school's summer vacation was longer than I thought, so I wouldn't have been able to stand it if I didn't at least daydream about Mars. It was a long, long summer, and to make matters worse, I was holding down two jobs: the gas station in the afternoon, the convenience store at night. Sure, there were girls at each place, neither good nor bad, but since they were neither good nor bad, I was bored all the same. In comparison, did the rays of the sun that passed Mercury, Venus,

화성.

일터를 돌다보면 별의별 일들을 겪게 마련인데, 모쪼록 그해의 여름이 그러했단 생각이다. 주유소에선 시간당 천오백 원을, 편의점에선 천 원을 받았으므로 나는 늘 불만이 가득했다. 그게 그러니까, 시작 때완 달리 불만이 생기는 것이다. 편의점의 사장은 이러면서 세상을 배운다—라고 말했지만, 이천 원씩 받고 배우면 어디가 덧나나? 뭐야, 그럼 당신 자식에겐 왜 팍팍 주는데?를 떠나서—못해도 이천 원 정도의 일은 하고 있다고 나는 늘 생각했다. 글쎄 천 원이라니. 덥기만 덥고, 짜디짠, 지구.

코치 형이 가게를 찾아온 것은 그 무렵의 새벽이었다. 어떠냐? 좋아요. 편의점의 알바 역시 코치 형의 소개로 얻은 것이므로, 좋다고밖에는 말할 도리가 없었다. 지역의 알바 정보를 한 손에 쥐었다고 할까, 아무튼 그래서 후배들에게 일자릴 소개하고 요모조모 코치하길 좋아하는 인물이었다. 이 얼마나 요긴한가, 나는 카프리썬 하나를 꺼내 그에게 건넸다. 제 돈으로 사는 거예요.

and the neither-good-nor-bad stars to come all the way to Earth feel the way I did? Not too hot, far far-away Mars.

Going back and forth between jobs meant, it was only natural that all kinds of problems would arise, and that was exactly the case that summer. Since I was only making fifteen hundred *won* an hour at the gas station and a thousand *won* at the convenience store, I felt disgruntled all the time. I mean, it started off okay, but I became disgruntled. My boss at the convenience store said that's how you learn about the world, and I didn't feel I could ask him if it would really kill anyone for me to earn two thousand an hour while learning. And if what he said were true, how come he showered so much money on his own kids! I always thought that what I was doing was worth at least two thousand an hour. Seriously? Only a thousand? Way too hot, tight-fisted Earth.

It was around that time that Coach came to the store one morning. How's it going? Fine. Since he was the one who got me the gig at the convenience store, I had no choice but to say it was fine.

웃으며 말은 했지만 알고나 드세요, 제 인생의 이십오 분이랍니다. 시계를 쳐다보며 나는 생각했다. 지금 일하는 덴 사장이 꼴통이라서 말야…… 오늘도 여자애 허벅질 만졌지 뭐냐…… 나 참…… 그래도 되는 거냐? 되고 말고를 떠나, 허벅질 만진다면 시간당 만 원은 줘야 되는 게 아닌가, 나는 생각했다. 만지는 게 나쁜 게 아니다. 그러고 고작, 천 원을 주는 게 나쁜 짓이다. 적어도 나는, 그렇게 생각했다.

그건 그렇고, 너 푸시업 잘하냐? 푸시업이라뇨? 팔굽혀펴기 말이다. 무조건 잘한다고 나는 대답했다. 그래야 일자리가 생긴다는 건, 그때도 이미 기본 중의 기본이었다. 페이가 세. 시간당 삼천 원인데…… 대신 몸이 좀 힘들어. 삼천 원이요? 앞뒤 잴 것도 없이, 시간당 삼천 원이란 말에 귀가 확 뚫리는 기분이었다. 내 주변에 그런 고부가가치 산업이 존재하고 있었다니. 제의를 받은 사실만으로도, 갑자기 확, 고도산업사회의 일원으로 성장한 느낌이었다. 좋구말구요. 비하자면 수성과 금성과 지구를 지나, 비로소 화성에 다다른 태양광선이 바로 나 같은 기분일까? 있으나마나에 받으나마나, 지구

You could say he had the corner on all the part-time jobs in the area. He liked helping the younger guys find work and coaching them on this and that. Well, that's convenient, I thought, taking a Capri Sun out of the fridge compartment and handing it to him. It's on me. I said it with a smile, but as I glanced up at the clock, I thought to myself, I hope you know that's worth twenty-five minutes of my life. This place I'm working now, Coach said, the boss is an idiot... even today he touched a girl's thigh... Man! How do you get away with that? Right or wrong, if you touch a girl's thigh, I think you should at least pay her ten thousand an hour. There's nothing wrong with touching. But there is something wrong with only paying her a thousand. Anyway, that's what I thought.

Say, are you good at push-ups? Push-ups? You know, press-ups. I automatically said I was. Saying yes automatically was what you had to do to get a job, that was already the basics of the basics by then. The pay's good. Three thousand an hour... but it's a little hard on your body. Three thousand? That was all I needed to hear. The words *three thousand an hour* knocked the wax right out of my ears.

여 안녕.

그런 이유로, 나는 푸시맨이 되었다. 좋은 점은 전철을 공짜로 탄다는 것, 팔 힘이 세진다는 것, 게다가 다른 알바에 전혀 지장을 안 준다는 거야. 이를테면 여기 일을 마친 다음 슬슬 역에 나가 '한 딱가리' 하면 그만이란 거지. 깔끔해. 공사 소속이니 지불 확실하지, 운동이 되니 밥맛도 좋아, 그러니 잠 잘 자고 주유소 일도 계속 하고…… 코치 형의 코치가 쉬지 않고 이어진 것도 까닭은 까닭이었지만—다른 무엇보다 이유는 삼천 원이었다. 요는 짧고 굵게 번다, 이거군요. 그런가? 뭐…… 그런 식으로 생각할 수도 있을까 모르겠군. 코치 형이 어리둥절한 표정을 지었지만, 확실히 그런 식이라고, 나는 생각했다. 그것이 나의 산수(算數)다. 웃건 말건, 세상엔 그런 산수를 하며 살아야 하는 사람이 있다, 있게 마련이다.

미안하구나.

아버진 그렇게 얘기했다. 또 그 소리. 내가 일만 한다

To think that a business with such a high rate of return existed near me! Even just getting the offer made me feel like I had suddenly become a member of a highly advanced industrial society. No problem! In comparison, do the rays of the sun that reach Mars at last, after passing Mercury, Venus, and Earth, feel the way I do? So long, neither-good-nor-bad whether-I-get-it-or-not Earth!

That's the reason I became a pusher. The good thing is that you get to ride the subway for free, your arms get strong, and it doesn't even interfere with your other jobs. In other words, once you're done here, you head over to the station, take your turn in the ring, and that's it. Clean and easy. The pay is guaranteed since it's through the city, food tastes better because it's good exercise, and you can keep working at the gas station... Coach's non-stop coaching was reason enough, but more than anything, the reason was the three thousand *won*. So what you're saying is, it's like doing heavier weights with shorter sets? Yeah... I guess you could look at it that way. Coach looked confused, but I thought, that's definitely how it is. That was my arithmetic. Laugh if you want, but there are

하면 늘 같은 소리였다. 처음엔 들을 만했는데, 결국 들으나마나가 돼버린 지 오래다. 나이 마흔다섯에 시간당 삼천오백 원, 즉 그것이 아버지의 산수였다. 여하튼 무슨 상사(商社)에 다녔는데, 여하튼 〈무슨 상사〉라고밖에 말할 수 없는 직장이었다. 딱 한 번 나는 그곳을 찾아간 적이 있다. 중학생 때의 일인데 도시락을 갖다 주는 심부름이었다. 약도가 틀렸나? 엄마가 그려준 약도를 몇 번이고 확인하며, 근처의 골목을 서성이고 서성였다. 간신히 찾아낸 아버지의 사무실은—여하튼 그곳에 있기는 한, 그런 사무실이었다. 쥐들이 다닐 것 같은 어둑한 복도와, 형광등과, 칠이 벗겨진 목조의 문. 혹시 외국(外國)인가? 라는 생각이 들 만큼이나 〈을씨년〉스러운 곳이었다. 깜짝이야, 그런 단어가 머릿속에 있었다니. 넉넉한 환경은 아니어도, 제법 메탈리카 같은 걸 듣던 시절이었다. 그래도 세상은 뭔가 ESP 플라잉브이(메탈리카가 사용한 기타의 모델명)와 같은 게 아닐까, 막연한 생각을 나는 했었다. 했는데, 해서 문을 열고 들어서자 꼬박꼬박 도시락만 먹어온 얼굴의 아버지가 가냘픈 표정으로 사무를 보고 있었다. 아버지, 저 왔어요.

people in this world who have to do that kind of arithmetic to get by. There just are.

I'm sorry.

That's what Dad always said. There he goes again. It was the same every time I said I'd started working. I liked hearing it the first time, but now it had lost all meaning. Thirty five hundred *won* an hour at the age of forty-five, that was Dad's arithmetic. In any case, he worked in some trading office, the kind of place you just called "The Office." Just once, I went to see him there. It was back when I was in middle school and Mom had sent me to deliver his lunch. Is this map right? I kept checking the map Mom had drawn for me and wandering all over the neighboring alleyways. I barely managed to track down Dad's office. Anyway, it was just sort of there, one of those types of offices: fluorescent lights, paint peeling off the wooden door, a dimly lit hallway that looked like it was frequented by mice. It almost made you wonder if you'd stumbled into some foreign country, it was such a "godforsaken" place. That's weird, I thought, where did that word come from? Though

원래 좀 노는 편이었는데, 이상하게 그날 이후 나는 조용한 소년이 되어버렸다. 뭐랄까, 그때는 몰랐지만 그 순간 마음속에 〈나의 산수〉와 같은 게 생겨났기 때문이었다. 아마도 그랬다고, 지금의 나는 생각한다. 그것은 슬픈 일도 기쁜 일도 아니었으며, 누구를 원망할 성질의 것은 더더욱 아니었다. 그저, 말 그대로 수(數)였던 것이다. 말수가 줄어든 대신, 나는 열심히 알바를 하고 돈을 모으기 시작했다. 야, 세상은 한 방이야. 어울리던 친구들이 안쓰럽단 투로 말했지만, 나는 알고 있었다. 결국 이들도, 같은 산수를 할 수밖에 없단 사실을. 넌 뭘 할 건데? 나? 글쎄 요샌 연예계가 어떨까 싶어.

인간에겐 누구나 자신만의 산수가 있다. 그리고 언젠가는 그것을 발견하게 마련이다. 물론 세상엔 수학(數學) 정도가 필요한 인생도 있겠지만, 대부분의 삶은 산수에서 끝장이다. 즉 높은 가지의 잎을 따먹듯—균등하고 소소한 돈을 가까스로 더하고 빼다보면, 어느새 삶은 저물기 마련이다, 디 엔드다. 어쩌면 그날 나는 〈아버지의 산수〉를 목격했거나, 그 연산(演算)의 답을 보았거나, 혹 그것을 고스란히 물려받았는지도 모를 일이

we weren't well off or anything, I listened to a lot of Metallica and stuff back then. Won't life be kind of like an ESP Flying V (the guitar model used by Metallica)? I used to wonder vaguely. Yeah, that's how I used to think, but then I opened the door and saw my dad sitting at his desk with the wan expression of a man who had duly eaten a packed lunch every single day. Dad, I'm here.

I used to be the playful type, but after that day, oddly enough, I turned into a quiet kid. I didn't realize why at the time, but I guess it was because some sense of my own arithmetic popped up inside me. Looking back on it now, I think that's what happened. It wasn't anything to be happy or sad about, and definitely wasn't anything to feel bitter about. It was literally just a matter of numbers. Instead of running off at the mouth, I started working hard at part-time jobs and saving up money. Go for the big payoff. My friends sounded like they pitied me, but I knew the drill. In the end, they, too, would have to do the same arithmetic. So what are you gonna do? Me? I dunno, lately I've been thinking maybe something in showbiz.

다. 즉 그런 셈이었다. 도시락을 건네주고, 산수를 받는다. 도시락을 건네주고, 산수를 받았다. 그리고 느낌만으로 〈아버지 돈 좀 줘〉와 같은 말을 두 번 다시 하지 않는 인간이 되었다.

참으로, 나의 산수란.

미안하구나. 아버지는 그렇게 얘기했지만, 아버지, 이건 나의 산수예요 라고 나는 생각했다. 정기적금 정기적금, 또 한 통의 자유적금. 시급 천오백 원과 천 원이 따로따로 쌓여가는 통장들을 생각하면, 세상에 힘든 일은 없었다. 말할 것 같으면, 내 주변은 주로 그랬다. 코치 형만 해도 통장이 다섯 개다. 코치 형네엔 아버지가 없지만, 우리 집처럼 병든 할머니가 있는 것도 아니었다. 쌤쌤이다. 어머닌 식당일을, 그 외엔 말을 안 해 더 이상은 모르겠다. 들은 바, 중학생 때의 코치 형은 본드로 유명한 소년이었다, 한다. 무렵엔 그 말을 도저히 믿을 수 없었다. 그래, 누구나 자신의 산수를 가지고 살아가는 거겠지. 그러니까

When it comes to people, everybody has their own arithmetic. And it's a sure thing that one day you'll discover this. Of course in this world, there are some lives that need higher mathematics, but for most, it ends at arithmetic. Like picking and eating a leaf from the next highest branch, you painfully add to and subtract from your tiny, unchanging pile of money, until one day your life draws to a close: The End. Maybe that day I saw Dad's Arithmetic with my own eyes, or saw the answer to the arithmetic operation or, who knows, maybe I even inherited it in its entirety. That was pretty much the case. Hand him his lunch, take his arithmetic. Handed him his lunch, took his arithmetic. And from what I sensed, I turned into someone who never let the words "Dad, can I have some money" cross his lips again.

Seriously, that arithmetic of mine.

I'm sorry. Dad always said that, but I thought, Dad, this is my arithmetic. Installment savings, installment savings, and another savings account. When I thought about my hourly wages of fifteen hundred *won* and a thousand *won* each growing bit

나의, 산수.

지금 열차가 들어오고 있습니다

승객 여러분들은 안전선 밖으로 물러나 주셔야겠지만, 그게 될 리가 없는 것이다. 승객들은 모두 전철을 타야 하고, 전철엔 이미 탈 자리가 없다. 타지 않으면, 늦는다. 신체의 안전선은 이곳이지만, 삶의 안전선은 전철 속이다. 당신이라면, 어떤 곳을 택하겠는가.

처음 열차가 들어오던 그 순간을 나는 잊을 수 없다. 그러니까 열차라기보다는, 공포스러울 정도의 거대한 동물이 파아, 하아, 플랫폼에 기어와 마치 구토물을 쏟아내듯 옆구리를 찢고 사람들을 토해냈다. 아아, 절로 신음이 새어나왔다. 뭔가 댐 같은 것이 무너지는 광경이었고, 눈과 귀와 코를 통해 머리 속 가득 구토물이 차오르는 느낌이었다. 야! 코치 형이 고함을 질러주지 않았으면, 나는 아마도 놈의 먹이가 되었을 테지. 정신이 들고 보니, 놈의 옆구리가 흥건히 고여 있던 구토물을

by bit in those accounts, there was no such thing as hard work. I guess you could say, that's how it was for everyone I knew. Even Coach had five accounts of his own. Coach didn't have a dad, but then again, he didn't have a sick grandma at home either. Same, same. His mom worked in a restaurant, and I don't know the rest because he never talked about it. I'd heard that Coach was known for being a glue sniffer in middle school but I couldn't believe a word of it at the time. Well, everybody has to get by on their own arithmetic. That's why I say,

MY arithmetic.

The Train Is Now Arriving

Passengers, please stand behind the yellow line. Which is impossible. Everyone has to get on the train, but there's no more room. If you don't get on, you'll be late. The body's yellow line may be here, but life's yellow line is inside the train. Which one would you choose?

다시금 빨아들이고 있었다. 발전(發電)이라도 일어날 기세였다. 힘! 그때 코치 형이 고함을 질렀다. 해서, 엉겁결에—영차, 영차 무언가 물컹하거나 무언가 딱딱한 것들을 마구마구 밀어 넣긴 했지만 그것이 무엇이었는지는 지금도 기억나지 않는다. 아니, 어찌 내 입으로 그것이 인류(人類)였다고 말할 수 있겠는가.

정신 차려. 열차가 출발하자 코치 형이 다가와 단단히 주의를 주었다. 네. 심호흡을 크게 했지만 다리가 떨리긴 마찬가지였다. 저 사람들을 사람이라고 생각하지 마. 화물이나, 뭐 그런 걸로 생각하란 말이야. 알겠니? 알겠지? 알겠지, 에서 다시 열차가 들어왔으므로, 나는 새로이 전열을 가다듬었다. 파아, 하아. 의정부 행이었던 두 번째 열차는, 아마도 두 배의 사람들이 쏟아져 나오는 느낌이었다. 이건 마치, 전 인류가 아닌가.

그렇게 한 시간이 지나갔다. 정신을 차리고 보니 나는 안전선 밖의, 그러니까, 〈물러서 주시기 바랍니다〉 정도의 지점에 주저앉아 있었다. 그리고 눈앞에는—세 개의 넥타이핀과 두 개의 단추, 더불어 부러진 안경다리

I'll never forget that moment when the first train arrived. I mean, not a train, but a freakishly huge animal that crawled up to the platform and wheezed, *paah, haah*, then ripped its sides open and spewed out people like it was vomiting. *Argh*, I moaned involuntarily. It looked like a dam breaking, and I could feel the inside of my head filling with vomit through my eyes, ears, and nose. Hey! If Coach hadn't yelled at me, I might have fallen prey to the beast. When I snapped out of it, I saw that the creature's sides were sucking the pool of vomit back up. It did so with enough force to have generated electricity. Just then, Coach yelled. *Push!* So, despite myself and with a heave ho, I began shoving in spongy things, hard things, but even now I couldn't tell you what they were. Seriously, how dare I say they were human beings?

As the train left, Coach came up and gave me a firm warning. Keep it together. Yes, sir. I took a deep breath, but my legs shook all the same. Don't think of them as people. Think of them as cargo, or something. Got it? Got it? Just as he said, "Got it?" again, another train was pulling in, so I braced myself once more. *Paah, haah*. The train bound for

가 부상병의 목발처럼 뒹굴고 있었다. 뿔테였다. 인류의 분실물들을 수거하며, 나는 비로소 온몸이 땀으로 젖어 있다는 사실을 알 수 있었다. 그러니까, 화성인들은 좋겠다. 참, 좋겠다.

일주일이 그런 식으로 지나갔다. 아침이면 전 인류의 참상을 목격하고, 오전의 짧은 잠, 이어지는 주유소 알바와 밤의 편의점. 온종일 머리 어깨 무릎 발 무릎 발이 아프더니, 다음날엔 머리 어깨 무릎 발 무릎 발 무릎이 아팠고, 그 다음날엔 머리 어깨 발 무릎 발 머리 어깨 무릎 귀 코 귀까지가 아프다고 할 정도로, 온몸이 아파왔다. 이건…… 시간당 삼만 원은 받아야 하는 게 아닌가. 나는 다시 불만에 사로잡혔지만, 지금 관두면 억울하지 않니? 코치 형의 코치도 과연 옳은 말이다 싶어 이를 악물고 출근을 계속했다. 어쩌면 피라미드의 건설 비결도 〈억울함〉이었는지 모른다. 지금 관두면 너무 억울해. 아마도 노예들의 산수란, 보다 그런 것이었겠지.

이상하게 이를 악물고 일을 하다 보니, 그럭저럭 일에도 재미가 붙기 시작했다. 머리 어깨 무릎 발 무릎 발도

Uijeongbu threw up twice as many people. It was like all of humanity this time.

It went on for an hour. When I came to my senses, I was slumped outside the yellow line, i.e. the Please Stand Behind point. And before my eyes—three tiepins, two buttons, and the broken leg of a pair of glasses like the crutch of an injured soldier were lying there. The glasses were horn-rimmed. Collecting the lost articles of mankind, I realized suddenly that my entire body was soaked in sweat. Like I said, must be nice to be a Martian. Seriously, nice.

A week went by. Witness the tragedy of mankind by morning, catnap before noon, then work the gas station in the afternoon and the convenience store at night. My body hurt so much, you could say my head, shoulders, knees and toes, knees and toes ached all day, then the next day, my head, shoulders, knees and toes, knees and toes, and knees ached, and then after that, it was head, shoulders, toes, knees and toes, head, shoulders, knees and ears, nose, ears. This... shouldn't it at least pay thirty thousand *won* an hour? I felt dis-

더 이상 아프거나 쑤시지 않았고, 이거야 원, 나는 즐거웠다. 여름의 새벽은 신선했고, 개봉역의 입구에선 대개 코치 형이 담배를 물고 서 있었다. 그리고 큰형(매표소의 직원을 코치 형은 큰형이라 불렀다)에게서 무임권을 얻는다. 얻고, 플랫폼에 올라선 우리는 어떤 특권처럼—라인의 맨 앞쪽에서 열차를 기다린다. 예전의 나였다면, 아마도 어김없이 여덟 번째 출구(집에서 최단 거리여서 항상 서게 되는 위치)의 대기선에서 열차를 기다렸겠지만, 그해 여름 나는 분명히 〈푸시맨〉이었다. 코치 형을 따라 공손히 인사를 하면, 기관사들은 대개 기관사석이나 차장석의 문을 열어주었다. 이 얼마나, 근사한 일인가.

사람들은 우리를 전설이라 부른다. 훈시랄까, 아니면 설교랄까—숙직실에서 〈감독〉의 얘기를 듣는 것도 보통 재미가 아니었다. 나이와 경력, 팔뚝의 힘, 투철한 직업관, 그리고 개똥철학…… 모든 면에서 최고참인 그를 우리는 감독이라 불렀다. 실제 푸시맨들의 조장 역을 맡고 있었으므로 감독의 말은 곧 빛이자 생명, 까지는 아니고 아, 예예 였다. 그럼요 그럼요, 요지는 늘—우리가 국가 경제의 중추라는 둥, 교통대란을 막는 네덜란드의 소년(거 왜, 댐을 막았다는)이라는 둥, 하물며 우리

gruntled again, but Coach asked, wouldn't it be a shame to quit now? Coach's coaching made sense, so I gritted my teeth and kept going to work. Maybe that's the secret behind the pyramids. Would be a shame to quit now. Maybe, just maybe, that was the slaves' arithmetic.

Oddly enough, once I gritted my teeth and gave it my all, the work began to have a fun of its own. My head, shoulders, knees and toes, knees and toes no longer hurt or ached, and, what the hell, I was having a good time. The early summer mornings were fresh and cool, and Coach was usually smoking a cigarette by the Gaebong Station entrance. We would get free tickets from Eldest Brother (that's what Coach called the ticket booth guy). Then, standing on the platform, we would wait for the train at the very front of the line—as if it were a privilege. The old me would have automatically waited in line near the eighth exit (where I always stood because it was the shortest distance from my house), but that summer I was a pusher. Following Coach's cue, we would bow respectfully to the subway drivers, and they would usually open the door to the engineer's seat or the conductor's seat for

업계의 신화라는 둥. 아, 예예.

시급 삼천 원을 받으며 네덜란드의 소년이 되고 싶진 않았지만, 모두가 수긍하는 감독의 말이 있었다. 그것은 우리가 '일당 백'이라는 사실이었다. 정예, 정예, 감독은 늘 일당 백의 정예가 아니고선 신도림역 푸시맨의 자격이 없다고 설교를 늘어놓았다. 해서 사람을 미는 요령, 틈 사이에 발이 빠진 사람의 구출 요령, 또 열차 한 량의 정원이랄까 그런 것—또 그런가 하면, 갑자기 요새 '오 예스'란 과자가 나왔는데 맛있더라, 너는 '쵸코파이'와 '오 예스' 중 어떤 게 맛있냐고 물어서 사람을 당황케 하는 재주를 가지고 있었다. 하하, 예예.

그리고 많은 일들이 있었다. 어른들 사이에 파묻혀 기절한 어린이가 있었고 도대체 이 시간에 애를 태워 보내는 부모가 어딨어! 흥분한 감독이 부모를 찾았지만, 그런 부모 따위가 열차에 탔을 리 없었다. 숙직실에서 눈을 뜬 어린이는 수학경시대회에 가야 하는데, 엄마에게 혼나는데, 라며 눈물을 흘렸다. 감독은 부천에서 왔다는 그 어린이에게 자신의 돈으로 콜라와 오 예스를

us. How cool was that?

People hail us as legends. I even liked listening to the talks Chief gave in the night duty room—you could call them instructions, or rather, sermons. Age, experience, arm strength, cast-iron work ethic, and mongrel philosophy... our leader in every respect, we called him Chief. Since he was in charge of the pushers, his word wasn't quite our light and life, but it was: Sir! Yes, sir! Of course, of course! And the point stayed the same—we were the backbone of the nation's economy, the Dutch boy (you know, the one who plugged the dike) preventing traffic chaos, not to mention legends of the trade. Sir! Yes, sir!

Although we had no intention of playing the Dutch boy for three thousand *won* an hour, there was one thing the Chief said that we all agreed with: we were "worth a hundred men each." Best of the best, Chief always preached on and on that those who were not worth-a-hundred, best-of-the-best were not worthy of the post of pusher at Sindorim Station. He gave us tips on how to push people, how to rescue a person whose foot got

사주었다. 막내가 좀 갔다 와라. 감독의, 인생의 삼십 분을 건네받으며 나는 평소와 달리 아, 네, 라고 짧게 끊어 대답했다.

제발…… 지각이에요. 그런 여자도 있었다. 가능한 등이나 어깨를…… 즉 여성의 몸을 함부로 밀기가 아직은 곤란했던 무렵이었다. 그래서 머뭇머뭇 그만 두 대의 열차를 놓쳐버렸다. 눈앞에서 울음을 터뜨리는데, 난감해서 견딜 수 없었다. 해서 코치 형을 불렀다. 그리고 의정부 행이 들어왔는데, 어찌나 사람이 많은지 코치 형조차 여자를 넣는 데 실패했다. 결국 여자를 넣은 것은 감독이었다. 열차 쪽을 보지 마시고, 저를 보세요 저를. 그리고 척 보기에도 가슴 같은 곳을 막 눌러, 쑤욱 밀어 넣었다. 잘 들어. 남자는 앞을 보게 해야 잘 들어가고, 여자는 돌아서게 해야 잘 들어가. 알았지? 왜 그런 겁니까? 하여튼 그래.

푸시맨 하나가 열차 속에 딸려들어간 적도 있었다. 뒤에 있던 사람들에게 떠밀려, 순식간에 일어난 일이었다. 일어날 수 있는 일이 일어난 것뿐이었는데, 문제는

caught in the gap, or how many people one train was supposed to hold—and on top of that, he had a knack for catching a person off guard by suddenly saying something like, there's a new cookie called Oh Yes, it's really good, and then asking you, which do you like better, Choco Pie or Oh Yes? Ha, ha, sir, yes, sir!

A lot of things happened. A kid sandwiched in a crowd of adults blacked out. Who in the world would let their kid ride the subway at this time of day? Chief muttered, all worked up and looking around for the kid's parents, but parents like that weren't the type to be on the train themselves. When the kid opened his eyes in the night duty room, he burst into tears, bawling that he was supposed to be at a math contest so he was really going to get it from his mom. Chief offered to buy the kid, who said he lived in Bucheon, a Coke and an Oh Yes with his own money. The youngest guy should go get it, he said. I took the thirty minutes of his, Chief's, life that he handed me and surprised myself by answering briskly, yes, sir!

Please... I'm late. A girl said that to me one day.

그 다음이었다. 승객 한 사람이 시비를 걸며 머리를 쥐어박은 것이다. 이유는 간단했다. 평소 이놈들이 싸가지 없이 사람을 민다는 것이었다. 맞은 애도 보통 성질은 아니어서, 그만 사건이 커지고 말았다. 결과는 집단구타였다. 전치 삼 주. 도망친 승객들은 아무도 잡히지 않았고, 결국 그 친구는 자신의 돈으로 앞니를 해 넣어야 했다. 그리고 아무도, 그 친구를 볼 수 없었다.

대신 나는, 여러 명의 변태를 볼 수 있었다. 또 보진 못해도, 여성의 비명이나 그런 걸 통해 차량의 어느 언저리에 변태가 있음을 알 수 있었다. 한번은 여자의 치마에 정액을 묻히던 사십대가 현장에서 붙잡혔다. 손을 움직일 틈이 있었을까? 그 속에서 그런 짓을 한 것도, 그 와중에 그런 인간을 붙잡은 것도 모두가 대단한 일이라고 나는 생각했다. 많아, 굉장히 많아. 코치 형이 고개를 가로저었다. 그런데 형…… 아무리 그게 좋다 쳐도…… 과연 저 속에 타고 싶을까요? 그건 모르지. 변태의 속사정을 어떻게 알겠니? 갓 경찰로 부임한 친구가 있거든. 그 친구가 그러는데 하루는 알몸의 삼십대 남자가 화단에서 꽃을 먹고 있다는 신고를 받았다지 뭐

Just the back or shoulders... I was still having a hard time pushing a woman's body any which way. So I hesitated while two trains went by. She started crying right in front of me; it was too much for me to take. So I called for Coach. A train for Uijeongbu pulled in, but it was so full that even Coach couldn't squeeze her in. In the end, Chief was the one who got her in. Don't look at the train. Here, look at me. I saw that he had no problem pushing her on the chest and stuff and shoved her in easily. Listen up. Guys go in easier facing front, and girls facing back. Got it? Why is that? Doesn't matter, it just is.

One time, one of the pushers got swept on to the train. He was shoved by the passengers behind him, and it happened in a flash. It was just something that could happen any time, but the problem was what happened next. One of the passengers picked a fight with him and punched him in the head. The reason was simple. He thought pushers were all jerks. The pusher he punched wasn't all that nice either, so the fight got bigger. It ended in a dog pile. Took the pusher three weeks to recover. None of the passengers that ran off were caught, so the guy had to pay for his new front

냐? 꽃, 이라구요? 응, 꽃.

사정(射精)을 하다 붙잡힌 남자는 상습범으로 밝혀졌다. 과묵한 인상에 피부가 매우 흰, 점이 많은 얼굴이었다. 살이 찐 목과 근처의 주름을 따라 연신 땀이 흘러내렸다. 변태 주제에 하와이라도 다녀온 모양이지? 감독이 빈정댔지만 그는 결코 얼굴을 들지 않았다. 다른 이유는 없고, 그저 곁에 선 경찰의 제복에 비해 그의 꽃무늬 알로하셔츠가 지나치게 아름답기도 해서—불현듯 나는 이런 생각을 하게 되었다. 하와이에도 전철이 있을까? 하와이에도 화단에서 꽃을 먹는 알몸의 남자가 있을까? 그리고 하와이에도, 푸시맨들이 있을까? 지구는 둥그니까 자꾸 걸어 나가면, 그러니까 알로하, 오에.

결국 모든 인간은 상습범이 아닐까, 나는 생각했다. 상습적으로 전철을 타고, 상습적으로 일을 하고, 상습적으로 밥을 먹고, 상습적으로 돈을 벌고, 상습적으로 놀고, 상습적으로 남을 괴롭히고, 상습적으로 거짓말을 하고, 상습적으로 착각을 하고, 상습적으로 사람을 만나고, 상습적으로 대화를 나누고, 상습적으로 회의를

teeth with his own money. After that, we never saw him again.

As for me, I saw a lot of perverts. And even when I didn't see one, I could tell by the sound of a woman shrieking that there was a pervert somewhere in the train car. Once, a guy in his forties was caught red-handed, smearing semen on a woman's skirt. How did he have room to move his hands? I thought it was amazing, both him trying something like that in there, and then us managing to catch the guy. There're a lot of them, a whole lot. Coach shook his head. But Coach... no matter how badly they want to do it... why would they want to get on that crowded train? I have no idea. Who knows what perverts are thinking? I have this friend who just became a cop. He said that one day he got a report of a thirty-year-old naked guy eating flowers in a garden. Did you say flowers? Yup, flowers.

The man who got caught ejaculating turned out to be a habitual offender. His face was pasty and covered in moles, and he had a quiet look about him. Sweat kept dripping along the folds of his fat

열고, 상습적인 교육을 받고, 상습적으로 머리 어깨 무릎 발 무릎 발이 아프고, 상습적으로 외롭고, 상습적으로 섹스를 하고, 상습적으로 잠을 잔다. 그리고 상습적으로, 죽는다. 승일아. 온몸으로 밀어, 온몸으로! 나는 다시 사람들을 밀기 시작했다. 온몸으로, 상습적으로.

8월이 되면서 점점 이력이랄까, 그런 게 붙기 시작했다. 게다가 신참들이 늘어났다. 집단폭행의 여파도 여파였고, 몸이 힘든 만큼 일을 관두는 숫자도 상당했기 때문이었다. 결국 나는 전철의 중심 쪽으로 점점 위치를 옮겨야 했다. 갈수록 사람들은 많아지고, 밀수록 사람들은 밀려 나왔다. 물론 대우가 좋아지고, 다들 나의 근성을 인정하는 분위기라 어려움은 덜했지만, 정작 어려운 문제는 그런 것이 아니었다. 물론

돈도 좋지만

아침마다 수많은 사람들의 고통을 목격하는 일이 점점 하나의 스트레스로 변해갔다. 가까스로 문이 닫히면, 으레 유리창에 밀착된 누군가의 얼굴과 대면하기

neck. Looks like the pervert's been to Hawaii or something, Chief said, making fun of him, but the guy never raised his head. For no other reason, just that his flowery aloha shirt next to the uniform on the cop standing next to him looked so beautiful, I was struck by a sudden thought: Are there subways in Hawaii, too? Is there a stark naked guy eating flowers in a garden in Hawaii, too? And in Hawaii, are there pushers? Since the earth is round, if you keep on walking, then it's like, Aloha 'Oe.

Maybe in the end all human beings are habitual offenders, I thought. We habitually ride the subway, habitually work, habitually eat meals, habitually make money, habitually have fun, habitually harass others, habitually lie, habitually misunderstand, habitually hang out, habitually converse, habitually hold meetings, habitually get educated, habitually ache in our head, shoulders, knees and toes, knees and toes, habitually feel lonely, habitually have sex, habitually sleep, and, habitually, die. Seung-il! Put your whole body into it, your whole body! I started pushing people again. With my whole body, habitually.

일쑤였다. 이런 풍선을 봤나, 터질 듯 짓눌린 볼과 입술을, 또 납작해진 돼지코를 보고 처음엔 배를 잡고 웃었지만, 날이 갈수록 웃음은 사라져 갔다. 좋아요, 다 좋은데 그러니까 당신이 기억하는 인류의 얼굴을 말해보란 얘기야. 화성의 누군가로부터 그런 추궁을 받는다면 나는 적잖이 고통스러울 것만 같았다. 다른 행성의 존재에게 알려주기엔, 인류의 몽따주는 얼마나 슬픈 것인가. 지금 열차가 들어오고 있습니다. 파아, 하아. 그래 전철만 다녀라, 은하철도 같은 건 아예 생각지도 말아야 한다. 지금 이대로의, 인류라면 말이다.

결국 또 한 칸 신참에게 자리가 밀려, 나는 여덟 번째 승강구를 맡게 되었다. 〈8〉. 노란색으로 박혀 있는 양각의 숫자를 내려다보다, 나는 문득 〈나의 산수〉를 떠올렸다. 왜, 이렇게 살아야 하나, 얼핏 바보 같은 생각이 들었지만 산수란 말 그대로 수(數)에 불과한 것이라고, 스스로를 다독여주었다. 유난히 머리 어깨 무릎 발, 무릎 발이 무겁게 느껴지는 아침이었다. 파아, 하아. 그리고 여전히 열차가 들어오고, 문이 열리고, 누군가가 압력에 의해 튕겨 나왔는데, 그런가 했는데

By August, I'd started getting the hang of things. Plus we kept getting more newbies. That was partly fallout from the fight on the train, and partly because the job was so tough that a lot of guys quit. As a result, I had to keep making my way closer to the center of the trains. There were more and more people, and the more I pushed, the more people poured out. Of course, I was treated better, and there were fewer difficulties since everyone saw that I had guts, but the real problem lay elsewhere. Of course,

the money was good, but

witnessing the suffering of countless people every morning was turning into one big headache. Each time the doors squeaked closed, I would be confronted with someone's face pressed up against the glass. Ever seen a balloon like that? I laughed until my stomach hurt at first to see all those squashed cheeks and lips about to burst and the flattened piggy noses, but as the days went on, the laughter went away. Fine, that's all fine, but what I want to hear about is the face of humanity as you remember it! If someone from Mars were to inter-

아버지였다.

뭐랄까, 일이 끝나면—옷을 전부 벗어 던지고 근처의 화단으로 가 꽃이라도 뜯어먹고 싶은 심정이었다. 아, 아버지…… 그런 말을 했는지 안 했는지에 대해선 잘 기억이 나지 않는다. 다만 신설역까지 가야 하는 아버지를, 마치 처음 여자의 몸을 밀 때처럼, 그래서 잘, 못 밀고, 그래도 좀 밀었는데, 잘, 안 들어가고, 그랬다. 열차의 문이 닫혔다. 파아, 하아. 상체를 구부려 무릎에 손을 얹고, 나는 제법 숨을 몰아쉬었다. 파아, 하아. 어색한 표정으로 아버지는 어색해진 넥타이를 고쳐 매고 서 계셨다. 그리고 잠깐, 넥타이를 맬 만큼의 짧은 시간이 그러나 절대 풀리지 않을 매듭으로, 우리 둘 사이를 엮으며 지나갔다. 그것은 무척 이상한 체험이었다. 매듭의 바깥은 더없이 소란스러운데, 아버지와 나 사이엔 우주의 고요, 같은 것이 고여드는 기분이었다. 고요 속에서, 그러나 눈을 못 마주치는 우리의 결계를 넘어, 또 다시 안내방송이 흘러나왔다.

지금 열차가 들어오고 있습니다.

rogate me like that, I would feel pretty tortured. When it comes to telling beings from other planets about it, just how sad is this montage of humanity? The train is now arriving. *Paah, haah*. That's right, just ride the train, don't even think about the Galaxy Express. If this is what humanity is.

In the end, I got pushed down another space by a newbie, and found myself in charge of train door number eight. "8." Looking down at the number embossed in yellow, I thought of My Arithmetic. Why do I have to live this way? The foolish question popped into my mind but I consoled myself by saying, arithmetic is nothing more than numbers. My head, shoulders, knees and toes, knees and toes felt especially heavy that morning. *Paah, haah*. Then the train came in as usual, the doors slid open, and someone popped out of the train from the pressure of the other passengers:

It was Dad.

How can I put this? I felt like throwing off all my clothes once work was over and heading for the nearest garden to eat the flowers. D-Dad... I don't

이 부근의 어느 지붕

정말로, 지구가 돈다는 것을 알게 될 때가 있다. 일을 끝내고, 코치 형과 나란히 역사(驛舍)의 벤치에 앉아 있을 때가 더욱 그랬다. 다리를 길게 뻗고 머릴 좀 더 젖히면, 구름이 흘러가는 모습을 보게 되는 것이다. 약간의 현기증이 일기도 하지만, 즉 그래서 아, 지구가 돌고 있구나 라는 사실을 알게 된다. 그 느낌이 나는 좋았다. 그래서 자주, 나는 벤치에 몸을 뉘었다. 아버지를 만난 그 날도 그랬다.

승일아…… 이번엔 꼭 타야 한다. 그래서 세 번째 열차가 들어왔는데, 흐름이 좋지 않음을 간파한 감독이 미는 것을 도와주었다. 힘! 힘! 물론 그 화물이 나의 아버지임을 알 리도 없었지만 너무 거침없이 머릴 누르고, 막, 등을 팔굽으로 찧고, 밀고, 그랬다. 들어, 간다. 들어, 갔다. 들릴락 말락, 그리고 그 순간 아버지의 흉곽에서 어떤 미약한 소리 같은 것이 새어나오는 듯했다. 파아, 하아. 하지만 흉곽을 닫아 열차는 자신의 폐부 속에 아버지의 소릴 가두었고, 나는 더 이상 그 소리의 정체를 확인할 길이 없었다. 아무튼 고작, 러시아워 전철

remember whether I actually said that or not. He only had to get to Sinseol Station, but like the first time I had to push a woman, I just, I couldn't push him in, and I pushed a little anyway but he, he couldn't get in. The train doors closed. *Paah, haah*. I bent over and put my hands on my knees, trying to catch my breath. *Paah, haah*. Dad stood there adjusting his crooked tie with an awkward look on his face. Then briefly, a moment, barely long enough to tie a necktie, but with a knot so tight it would never come undone, passed between us, weaving us together. It was really odd. Outside the knot, it was as noisy as could be, but between my dad and me, something resembling the silence of outer space pooled between us. Inside that silence, the announcement came again, streaming over the walls of our sanctum where we could not meet each other's eyes.

The train is now arriving.

A Roof Somewhere Nearby

Sometimes you realize: the earth really is spin-

따위의 폐부에 갇힌 소리나 호흡, 그런 기포와도 같이
—답답하고

길고, 이상한 여름이었다. 형, 지구가 돌고 있어요. 그러냐? 뭔가 아버지에 대한 얘길 하고 싶었는데, 전혀 뜻밖의 말들만 튀어나왔다. 뭐 좀 마실래? 그리고 코치 형이 뽑아준 미린다 한 잔을 마시고 그걸로 끝이었다. 그 후로 제법, 자주, 나는 아버지를 보게 되었다. 서서히 서로에게 어떤 면역이 생겨나기도 했지만, 어떤 면역이 생겨도 자체가 즐거울 리 없는 만남이었다. 나는 때로, 제대로 아버지를 밀어 넣기도 했고, 그건 방학이 끝나갈 무렵이었고, 그런 날이면 언제나 음료수를 뽑아 마셨다. 저 멀리 구름은 흘러가고, 나는 목이 말랐다.

여름은 그렇게 지나갔다. 방학이 끝나면서 푸시맨 생활도 끝이 났고, 나는 다시 학교로 돌아왔다. 2학기가 시작된 학교는 몹시도 어수선한 분위기였다. 자리가 없어, 이구동성으로 선배들은 얘기했다. 이구동성이 아니어도, 세상의 불황을 누구나 알고 있었다. 자격증도 소용없고, 또, 정보산업고로 개명하면 취업률이 오를 거

ning. This was especially true after work, when Coach and I would sit side by side on a bench in the station. If I stretched my legs out and leaned my head back just a bit more, I could see the clouds outside drifting past. It made me a little dizzy, but it also made me realize, aha, the earth really is spinning. I liked that feeling. So, I lay on that bench a lot. I did it again the day I saw Dad.

Seung-il... I've got to get on the train this time. Two trains went by without Dad on them. When the third one came in, Chief, who had figured out that the current was against us, came over to help. Push! Push! Of course, he had no idea the cargo we were trying to load was my dad, but still, he was too rough, jamming his head down, ramming his elbows hard into Dad's back, shoving him in. GET in. GOT in. Just then a faint sound, now you hear it now you don't, seemed to seep out of Dad's thorax. *Paah, haah*. But the train snapped its own thorax shut, trapping Dad's sound deep inside its lungs, and I had no way of figuring out what that sound was. Anyway, it was just, like, an air bubble, a sound or a breath trapped inside the depths of, like, a train at rush hour—stifling

란 예상도 그러나 모두 루머에 불과한 것이었다. 선배들은 낙심했고, 여전히 구름은 흘러가고, 나는 목이 말랐다. 세상은 하나의 열차다. 한 량의 정원은 180명, 그러나 실은 400명이 타야만 한다—답답하고

길고, 이상한 여름은 끝이 났지만 대신 길고, 이상한 가을이 시작되었다. 그래서 9월이 끝나갈 무렵이었다. 엄마가 쓰러졌다. 상가 건물의 청소일을 오랫동안 해왔는데, 과로인지 뭔지 아무튼 쓰러졌다. 다행히 곧장 병원으로 옮겨졌고, 그러나 확실한 원인이 발견된 것은 아니었고, 일단은 신경인지 어딘지가 나빠질 만큼 나빠졌다는 얘기였다. 검사를 계속 해봅시다. 의사란 사람이, 그렇게 얘기했다. 검사는 계속 해야만 하겠지. 의사란 사람이, 그렇게 말했으니.

병실에 들어서자, 엄마의 손을 잡고 있는 아버지의 모습이 들어왔다. 엄만 어때? 대답 대신 아버지는 말없이 나를 바라보았다. 초원의 복판에서 갑자기 한쪽 다리를 못 쓰게 된 타조처럼—멍하고, 어두운 표정이었다. 실은 그동안 그나마 아주 잘 걸어왔다는, 아니 달려온 거

and long and strange, the summer was. Coach, the earth is spinning. Is it? I'd meant to say something about my dad, but that popped out of my mouth instead, totally unexpected. Coach offered to buy me a drink. So I drank the cup of Mirinda he got for me, and well, that was it. After that, I bumped into Dad pretty often. Slowly, we developed a kind of immunity towards each other, but even with that immunity, they were not happy encounters. Sometimes I managed to push him into the train just right, though it took me most of the summer to figure out how. On those days, I treated myself to a soda. The distant clouds drifted along, and well, I was thirsty.

That's how I spent my summer. When vacation ended, my days as a pusher ended as well, and I returned to school. The second semester of school was complete chaos. No jobs, the upperclassmen said in chorus. Chorus or not, everyone knew about the global recession. It didn't matter if you were qualified or not, and the assumption that changing the name of the school to Information Technology High School would raise the employment rate was nothing more than wishful thinking.

라는 생각이 나도 들었다. 사라질 엄마의 봉급, 여전한 할머니의 약값, 발생될 엄마의 치료비…… 아버지의 눈동자가 그토록 잿빛이었단 사실을 그때 처음 알았다. 뭐랄까, 전지가 떨어진 계산기의 꺼진 액정과 같은, 그런 잿빛이었다. 이제, 계산이 안 나온다. 나도, 계산이 서질 않았다. 불 꺼진 병원의 비상계단에서, 나는 코치 형에게 전화를 걸었다.

고학을 했던 담임은 비교적 이해심이 많은 인물이었다. 힘내거라. 내가 잘, 처리해주마. 해서 나는 1교시를 빼먹는 학생이 되었고, 덕분에 다시금 푸시맨 일을 하게 되었다. 나는 다시 전 인류의 물결을 감당해야 했고, 그 속에서 마치 부유하는 미역줄기와도 같은 아버지를 대면하기 일쑤였다. 맞다, 내 정신 좀 봐. 아버진 그때 점심을 어떻게 했을까? 굶은 걸까? 즉, 도시락의 무게만큼 가벼워진 아버지를 나는 밀고, 또 밀었다. 그 가을의 찬바람 속에서 내 손에 밀리던 아버지는 때로 웅크렸고, 때로 늘어졌으며, 때로 파닥이는, 그런 느낌이었다. 문득, 아침 바람 찬바람에 울고 가는 저, 기러기.

The seniors were losing heart, the clouds still drifted by, and I was thirsty. The world was one big train. It could only hold 180 people, but there were 400 who needed to get on—the stifling and

long, strange summer ended, but a long, strange autumn took its place. And just when September was on the verge of ending, Mom collapsed. She had been working for a long time as a cleaning lady at a shopping center, and she collapsed due to overwork or something. Luckily she was taken to the hospital right away, but they couldn't tell what was wrong with her, and for the time being, they said that her nerves or something were totally shot. Let's keep running tests. That's what he said, the doctor. I guess we'll just keep running tests then. Because that's what he said, the doctor.

When I went into her hospital room, I saw Dad holding Mom's hand. How is she? He stared at me wordlessly. It was a dark, dazed look—like an ostrich that's suddenly lost the use of one leg in the middle of a savanna. Actually, I thought that he had been walking, no, *running* along pretty well all that time. Mom's soon-to-be lost wages, her soon-to-

코치 형은 이런저런 알바 자리들을 서슴없이 나에게 인계해주었다. 고마워 형. 나는 목각(木刻)의 기러기 인형처럼 딱딱하게 고마움을 표했지만, 실은 울고 싶은 심정이었다. 새로 전지를 갈아 끼운 계산기의 액정에서, 새롭고 소소한 액수의 숫자들이 깜박깜박 빠르게 점멸하는 나날이었다. 그런 느낌이었다. 어느 날 거울을 보다가, 그런 잿빛의 눈동자를 나는 보았다. 아버지와 색이 같은 두 개의 동심원, 나는 결국 아버지의 연산(演算)이었다. 3.1415926535897…… 그리고

편의점의 사장과 트러블이 있었다. 돈을 안 줘서, 그래서 달라고 했는데, 점점 수작이 떼먹자는 수작이었다. 옥신각신하던 차에 그만 밀었는데, 나도 놀랄 만큼이나 한참을 날아갔다. 되려 허릴 다쳤다는 둥, 고소를 한다는 둥 난리를 쳤는데 이 역시 코치 형이 해결해주었다. 작은 소리로 잠시 얘길 했을 뿐인데, 사장이 나오더니 돈을 주었다. 아니, 뿌렸다. 줍자. 너무나 담담한 코치 형이 없었더라면, 또 한바탕 푸시를 할 뻔했었다. 액수는 맞니? 천 원이 모자라요. 저기, 천 원 모자랍니다. 코치 형이 크게 소리 질렀다.

be hospital bills, and Grandma's continuing medical bills... that was when I first realized that Dad's eyes were an ashy gray. I guess you could say they were the same shade of gray as the dead display on a calculator that's run out of batteries. Now, the numbers weren't coming up. I, too, couldn't get the figures to add up. In the unlit emergency stairwell of the hospital, I called Coach.

My homeroom teacher, who had also worked his way through school, was a pretty understanding guy. Hang in there. I'll take care of things for you. Thanks to him, I started skipping first period and became a pusher again. It was once again up to me to control that tidal wave of humanity, and I often saw my dad floating in there like a strand of seaweed. Oh right, where's my head at? What did Dad do for lunch then? Did he go hungry? I pushed Dad, who was one lunchbox lighter, again and again. Pushed by my hands, my father felt like he was sometimes crouching, sometimes drooping, sometimes flapping in the chilly autumn wind. A children's song suddenly came to mind: Morning wind, cold wind, that wild goose cries then flies away.

이상하게 그날 아침—나는 아버지를 아주 거칠게, 그렇게, 밀었다. 부끄럽지만, 그런 기분이었다. 아마도 땅바닥에 떨어진 돈을 한 장 한 장 주워서겠지, 그래서겠지. 애써 자위를 해봤자 기분이 좋을 리 없었다. 승일아, 잠깐만…… 잠깐만. 아주 잠깐, 아버지의 신음이 내 귓속을 비집고 들었지만 이상하게도 아무런 느낌이 없었다. 아버지, 잘 다녀오세요.

잘 다녀온 아버지는, 그러나 그날 밤 이런저런 사정들을 나에게 털어놓았다. 요는, 산수에 관한 것이었다. 점점 회사가 힘들어진다. 지금 다른 곳을 알아보고 있다. 미안한데, 당분간은 함께 좀 고생을 하자. 나는 하나도 힘들지 않다고, 얘기했다. 미안해하던 아버지를 다음날 또 마주쳤는데—미안한 마음에 제대로 밀지 못했다. 아버지, 잘 다녀오세요.

다릴 뻗고 고갤 젖히고, 그래서 구름이 흘러가는 걸 쳐다보며 나는 말했다. 형, 지구는 진짜 돌고 있어요. 그러냐? 이렇게 지구가 도는 게 느껴질 땐 말이죠, 문득 그런 생각이 들어요. 뭐가? 그러니까…… 정말 우주에

Coach never stopped trying to hook me up with this or that part-time gig. Thanks, Coach. So even though my thanks were as stiff as a carved wooden goose, I actually wanted to cry. The days passed by like new, insignificant figures flickering past on the display of a calculator with a fresh set of batteries. That's how it felt. One day when I looked in the mirror, I saw those ash-colored eyes. Two concentric circles the same shade as Dad's. I was my dad's arithmetic operation after all. 3.1415926 535897... And

there was trouble with my boss at the convenience store. He hadn't paid me, so I asked him to, and it became clearer and clearer that he was trying to stiff me. We squabbled over it, and I wound up shoving him. Even I was surprised to see how far he flew. He made a big stink about it, saying that his back hurt and he was going to press charges, but as always, Coach straightened it out for me. All he did was talk to him briefly in a low voice, and my boss came out and handed me the money. Or rather, he threw it at me. Let's pick it up. If oh-so-calm Coach hadn't been there, I might have gone for one more push. Is it all there? It's a

서…… 행성 위에서 살고 있는 거잖아요. 그래서? 이런 곳에서…… 왜 고작 이따위로 사는 걸까, 라고요. 잠시 침묵을 지키던 코치 형이 뭐 좀 마시자, 라며 자릴 일어섰다. 다릴 당기고 고갤 세워, 그래서 지구가 정지하고 나자 〈얼음 없음〉을 눌러 양이 더 많은 미린다 한 잔이 눈앞에 떠 있었다. 정지한 지구 위에서, 또, 지금 열차가 들어오고 있었다. 재밌는 얘기 하나 해줄까?

지금 들어온 열차가 출발하고 나자, 코치 형이 불쑥 그런 말을 뱉는 것이었다. 2교시도 빠지지 뭐. 해서 그 날따라, 나 역시 벤치에 눌러앉게 되었다. 그것은 재밌다기보다는, 어딘가 모르게 이상한 이야기였다. 본드를 한창 하던 때의 일이야. 여느 때처럼 끝까지 갔다 라고 생각했는데, 갑자기 내가 지붕 위에 떠 있는 거야. 신기한 게 아래엔 머릴 처박은 내 모습이 보이고, 그걸 바라보는 나 자신은 이상한 빛이 나는 거야. 나는 지금 죽은 건가, 그런 생각이 절로 들었지. 얼마나 무서웠나 몰라. 그래서 주위를 둘러보는데, 멀리 오류동 쪽에 아는 녀석 하나가 나처럼 떠 있는 거야. 진호라고, 그놈도 맨 본드하고 거기서 놀던 앤데…… 그래서 저놈도 죽은 건

thousand *won* short. Coach yelled, Hey, it's a thousand *won* short!

Oddly enough, I pushed Dad hard, really hard, that morning. I wasn't proud of it, but that's the mood I was in. Maybe it's because I had to pick the money up from the floor, one bill after the other. No matter how hard I tried to console myself, my mood didn't get any better. Seung-il, wait... wait. Hang on a second. Dad's groan pushed its way into my ear, but weirdly enough, I didn't feel a thing. Dad, come home safe.

Home safe, Dad opened up to me that night about this and that. In a word, it came down to arithmetic. The company is doing worse and worse. I'm looking for another job. I'm sorry, we each have to pull some weight for a while. I'm not having a hard time at all, I said. The next morning I ran into my apologetic dad again, but I couldn't push him properly for feeling sorry. Dad, come home safe.

I straightened out my legs and tilted my head back, watched the clouds drifting by and said,

가? 생각을 한 거지. 그리고 얼마쯤 지났을까? 다시 정신이 들고 깨어났어. 아니, 살아났다고 그때는 생각했지. 휴 하고 가슴을 쓸었는데, 정말 놀랄 일은 오후에 일어났어. 글쎄 진호 그놈이 날 찾아온 거야. 그리고 혹시 어젯밤에 본드 했냐고? 그래서 했다 했지. 그러자 공중에 떠 있는 자길 보지 않았냐고, 자긴 날 봤다고 그러는 거야. 나 참 얼마나 놀랐던지.

어쨌거나 그 일이 있고 나서, 나 완전히 딴사람이 돼버렸어. 본드도 끊고, 이유는 잘 몰라. 혹 언제라도 빠져나가, 이 부근의 어느 지붕에 떠 있으면 어쩌지? 그래서 열심히 사는 거 외엔 달리 방법이 없는 게 아닌가, 그런 생각도 들고. 이 부근의 어느 지붕요? 응.

이 부근의 어느 지붕

그렇습니까? 기린입니다

금성인들은 좋겠다. 그해 겨울엔 혹한이 닥쳐, 나는

Coach, the earth really is spinning. Oh yeah? When I feel the earth turning like this, it makes me think. What? Well... we really are living on a planet... in outer space. So? So I mean, why are we living like this? Coach was silent for a moment then stood up and said, Let's get a drink. I sat up and straightened my head to stop the earth from spinning, and there was a cup of Mirinda, extra full because he'd pushed the No Ice button, floating before my eyes. On the stopped earth, once again, a train was now arriving. Want to hear something funny?

After the now arriving train left, Coach suddenly threw that question out there. I figured, well, may as well skip second period, too, and wound up staying on the bench that day. His story was more weird than funny. This was back when I was sniffing glue all the time. As usual I thought I was as high as I was going to get, when suddenly I was floating over the roof. The funny thing was that I could see myself down below with my head shoved in the bag, and the me that was watching this was giving off a strange light. I thought, am I dead now? It was so scary. I looked around, and there was another guy floating like me way over by

늘 그런 상념에 젖고는 했다. 정보산업고(情報産業高)의 겨울방학은 생각보다 가혹해서, 그런 상념에라도 빠지지 않으면 견딜 수가 없었다. 긴긴 겨울, 여전히 나는 여러 일터를 전전했다. 이른 아침의 전철역에서 늦은 밤까지의 갈빗집 주방, 또 새벽엔 세 구역의 아파트를 돌며—신문을 돌렸다. 파아, 하아. 펴오르는 입김과 옷 속의 땀. 돌이켜보면, 부근의 어느 지붕에서 그런 자신의 모습을 내려다보는 기분이다. 금성인의, 시각 같다.

새벽의 전철은 늘 은하철도와 같은 느낌이었다. 그렇게 말해도 괜찮습니까? 금성의 누군가로부터 추궁을 받는다 해도, 과연 나는 그렇게 말할 수 있다. 새벽은 광활하고 캄캄했으며, 혹한의 공기는 언제나 거칠었다. 말 그대로의 천자문 집宇 집宙, 넓을洪 거칠荒, 그리고 나는, 혼자였다. 사람들은 모두 자고 있겠지, 사람들은 모두 무사하겠지. 구일과 구로를 지나 신도림으로 이어지는 선로의 어둠 속에서, 나는 늘 흔들리며 생각했다. 조금씩, 열차는 흔들렸고, 조금씩, 마음도 흔들렸다. 삶은, 세상은, 언제나 흔들리는 것이었다.

Oryu-dong. His name was Jin-ho, and he used to hang out there all the time, sniffing glue. So of course I thought, is he dead, too? Then, after a while, I came to and sobered up. Or, should I say I came back to life, which is what it felt like then. I breathed a sigh of relief, but later that afternoon, the craziest thing happened: Jin-ho came to see me. He asked if I'd been sniffing glue the night before. So I said I had. Then he asked if I'd seen him floating in the air. He said that he'd seen me. I was shocked.

After that, I became a totally different person. I quit sniffing glue, though I don't really know why. I mean, what if I left my body at some random moment and went floating over a roof somewhere nearby? So I thought, maybe there's no other way but to live life to the fullest. A roof somewhere nearby? Yeah,

a roof somewhere nearby.

Is That So? I'm A Giraffe

Must be nice to be a Venusian. Winter that year was so bitterly cold, I couldn't help thinking that

무사한 사람은 아무도 없었다. 알바를 정리한 코치 형은 떴다방의 직원이 되었는데, 불과 한 달 만에 사람이 달라졌다. 비록 중고지만 승용차를 구입했고, 돈의 씀씀이가 예전과 사뭇 달랐다. 우연히 길에서 만났는데, 내가 알던 코치 형과 유사한 인물이란 느낌만 간간이 들 뿐이었다. 유사한 것을 무사하다고 말할 순 없는 거니까, 즉 그런 거니까. 감독은 여전했지만, 그 역시도 무사한 것은 아니었다. 들리는 말로는 결혼 사기를 당했다는데, 그 후 열흘이나 무단결근을 했고, 그 후 다시금 출근을 했다. 본인은 어떤 말도 하지 않았고, 우리 역시 어떤 말도 하지 않았다. 사람은 배워야 해. 언젠가 불쑥 그런 말을 하길래 나는 아, 네, 라고 짧게 끊어 대답해주었다. 또 그런가 했더니, 갑자기 요즘 '칙촉'이란 게 나왔는데 먹어봤냐? 넌 '오 예스'와 '칙촉' 중 어떤 게 맛있냐고 묻길래—아, 예예. 그리고

그 겨울의 어느 날이었다.

아버지가 사라졌다.

way. The vocational high school's winter vacation was harsher than I expected, and I wouldn't have been able to stand it if I didn't at least daydream about Venus. All winter long, I was still working odd jobs. From the early morning subway station to the late night kitchen of the barbecue joint to the paper route of three apartment complexes at the crack of dawn. *Paah, haah*. The puff of my breath and the sweat beneath my clothes. Looking back, it felt like I was looking down at myself from a nearby roof. As if from their point of view, the Venusians.

The early morning subway was like the Galaxy Express. Are you comfortable with saying that? Even if I were grilled by someone from Venus, I would still be able to say that. The dawn was vast and dark, and the biting air was always harsh. Just as it says in the Thousand Character Classic, "The universe (宇宙) is vast (洪) and wild (荒)." And me, I was alone. Everyone is sleeping, everyone is safe, I assured myself as I swayed in the darkness of the rails past Guil and Guro to Sindorim. Inch by inch, the train swayed along, and inch by inch, so did my heart. Life, the world, was always in sway.

정말로 사라진 것이었다. 어떤 조짐도 보이지 않았고, 어떤 짐작도 할 수 없었다. 처음엔 사고가 아닌가 백방으로 뛰어다녔지만, 사고의 흔적은 어디에도 없었다. 행적에 대해 말해줄 수 있습니까? 아버지를 마지막으로 본 것은 나였으므로, 당연히 나는 그에 대해 할 말이 있었다. 그날 아침 전철역에서 만났습니다. 전철역에서요? 네, 아버지는 출근을 하는 길이었고, 저는 그곳에서 아르바이트를 하고 있었습니다. 종종 만나는 편인데, 늘 그랬듯 그날도 역시 아버지를 밀어드렸습니다. 뭐 특이한 점은 없었나요? 글쎄요…… 그러고 보니 〈잠깐만, 다음 걸 타자〉 하고 몸을 한 번 뺐습니다. 그런 적은 처음이었나요? 네, 아마도. 그래서 어떻게 했나요? 힘드신가보다, 라고 쉽게 생각했습니다. 그래서 다음 열차에 태워 보냈습니다. 순순히 타던가요? 그런, 편이었습니다.

그리고 그것이, 아버지의 마지막 모습이었다. 아버지는 회사에도 가지 않았고, 집으로도 오지 않았다. 말 그대로의, 실종. 경찰은 요즘 그런 사람들이 꽤 있다는 말로 나를 위로했지만, 그런 사람들이 꽤 있다고 해서 위

Not one of us was passing through life safely. Coach quit working part-time and got a job selling apartment shares on the sly, and in a month he was a changed person. He got a car, albeit a used one, and spent more money than before. I bumped into him once on the street, but he seemed like someone who only bore a passing resemblance to the Coach I used to know. But a passing resemblance to someone like Coach doesn't mean passing safely through life. Chief was the same as ever, but he wasn't passing safely through, either. Rumor was that he was hit by a marriage scam, and afterward he didn't show up for work for ten days. Then suddenly he was back. He didn't say anything, and neither did we. People have to learn. He would say that out of the blue, and I would respond briskly, yes, sir! When I thought he was done, he would suddenly ask me, have you tried the new cookie called Chic Choc? Which do you like better, Oh Yes or Chic Choc, he would ask—sir, yes, sir! Then

it happened one day that winter.

로가 될 리 없었다. 그 후의 기억은…… 잘 정리가 되지 않는다. 나는 아버지의 회사를 상대로 밀렸던 두 달 치 임금을 받아냈고, 이는 보통 힘든 일이 아니었고, 이런 저런 서류를 마련해 할머니를 관인 〈사랑의 집〉에 보내고, 이 또한 정말 까다롭고 힘든 일이었으며, 경찰서와 병원을 꾸준히 오고, 가고, 또 여전히 일을 했다, 해야만 했다. 때로 새벽의 전철에 지친 몸을 실으면, 그래서 나는 저 어둠 속의 누군가에게 몸을 떠밀리는 기분이었다. 밀지 마, 그만 밀라니까. 왜 세상은 온통 푸시인가. 왜 세상엔 〈푸시맨〉만 있고 〈풀맨〉이 없는 것인가. 그리고 왜, 이 열차는

삶은, 세상은, 언제나 흔들리는가. 그렇게

흔들리던 겨울이 가고, 봄이 왔다. 봄은 금성인과 화성인이 모두 부러워할 만큼이나 근사한 계절이었다. 끝내 아버지는 돌아오지 않았지만, 대신 어머니의 의식이 기적처럼 돌아왔다. 의식이 돌아왔다는 사실보다도, 퇴원을 할 수 있다는 사실이 기뻐 나는 울었다. 글쎄 그 정도의 서러운 이유라면, 누구나 눈물이 나오지 않았을

My dad disappeared.

He really was gone. He had shown no signs of leaving, and I'd had no way of guessing. At first I thought there'd been an accident and searched everywhere for him, but there was no trace of an accident anywhere. Can you tell us his last known whereabouts? I was the last one to see Dad, so of course I had something to say. I saw him that morning in the subway station. In the subway station? Yes, he was on his way to work and I was working part-time there. We ran into each other now and then, and that day as well I helped push him onto the train like I always did. Was there anything different about him? Hmm... come to think of it, he said, "Wait, I'll take the next one," and stood aside. He'd never done that before? No, I don't think so. So what did you do? I just thought he was tired. So I put him on the next train. He didn't resist? No, he didn't seem to.

And that was the last of Dad. He didn't show up at work, and he didn't come home. He was, literally, missing. The police tried to comfort me by saying there were a lot of people like him nowadays,

까? 이제 재활 치료만 받으면 됩니다. 의사란 사람이, 그렇게 얘기했다. 재활 치료만 받으면 되는 거겠지. 의사란 사람이, 그렇게 말했으니.

그렇게 우리 집은, 다시금 숨을 트고 있었다. 아버지가 사라졌지만 할머니란 짐을 덜게 된 까닭으로, 또 엄마가 스스로 자신의 병원비를 번 까닭으로 그대로, 그렇게. 근처의 지붕에서 지켜본다면, 아마도 그것은 잔디의 작은 싹이 움을 튼 모습과 비슷한 광경이었을 것이다. 살아, 있다. 무사하진 않았지만, 그래도 유사한 산수를 할 수 있단 것은 얼마나 큰 삶의 축복인가. 사라지기 전에, 사라지기 전에 말이다.

봄이 얼마나 완연한 날이었을까. 일을 마친 나는 잠깐 역사의 벤치에서 졸다가 깊고, 완연한 잠을 자버리고 말았다. 그리고 눈을 떴다. 목이 말랐다. 여느 때처럼 미린다 한 잔을 마시고 나자, 탄산수처럼 쏘는 느낌의 봄볕이 피부를 찔러왔다. 당연히 〈얼음 없음〉인 봄볕 속에는 그래서 그만큼의 온기가, 더 스며 있었다. 아아, 마치 기지개처럼 나는 다릴 뻗고 고갤 젖혔다. 여전히 구

but what's the use of knowing there were lots of people like my dad? My memory from then on... is all mixed up. I got the two months of paychecks from Dad's company that they had been withholding, which wasn't an easy thing to do, and I prepared all the documents to send Grandma to the "House of Love," an old folk's home, which was also a really complicated and difficult thing to do, went back and forth between the police station and the hospital, and went to work as usual, as I had to. Sometimes, when I put my tired body on the subway at dawn, I felt like someone was shoving me into the darkness. Don't push. Stop pushing, I said! Why is the world full of pushers? Why are there only pushers in this world and no pullers? And, why is this train,

life, the world, always swaying? In that way

the swaying winter passed, and spring came. That spring was enough to make both the Venusians and Martians jealous. Dad didn't come home, but Mom miraculously recovered consciousness. I cried with joy, not so much because she had recovered, but because she wouldn't have to stay in

름은 흘러가고 지구는 돌고, 그리고 다시 고개를 들었는데 건너편 플랫폼의 지붕 부근에 떠 있는 이상한 얼굴 하나가 눈에 들어왔다. 저것은 설마

기린이 아닌가. 그것은 정말 한 마리의 기린이었다. 기린은 단정한 차림새의 양복을 입고, 플랫폼의 이곳저곳을 천천히 거닐고 있었다. 오전의 역사는 한가했고, 아무리 한가해도 그렇지—사람들은 그럴 수도 있지 뭐, 의 표정으로 그다지 신경을 쓰지 않는 눈치였다. 이거야 원, 누군가 한 사람은 긴장을 해야 하는 게 아닌가, 란 생각으로 나는 기린을 예의, 주시했다. 끄덕끄덕, 머리를 흔들며 걷던 기린이 코너 근처의 벤치 앞에서 멈춰섰다. 그리고, 앉았다. 그것은 그리고, 앉았다 라고 해야 할 만큼이나 분리되고, 모션이 큰 동작이었다. 이상하게도 그 순간, 나는 기린이 아버지란 생각을 했다. 이유는 알 수 없지만, 그런 확신이 들었다. 나는 이미 통로를 뛰어가고 있었다. 사라지기 전에, 사라지기 전에.

다행히 기린은 꼼짝 않고 앉아 있었다. 주저주저 그 곁으로 다가간 나는, 주저주저 기린의 곁에 조심스레

the hospital anymore. Well, with as sad a reason as that, who wouldn't cry? Now she just needs physical therapy. That's what the doctor said. So she just needs physical therapy. Because that's what the doctor said.

That's how our family started breathing again. Because even though Dad had disappeared, we didn't have the burden of Grandma, and Mom was earning enough to pay her own medical bills. If you were watching us from a neighboring roof, it probably would have looked a lot like a small shoot sprouting out of a lawn. We were... alive. Far from passing through safely, but how great of a life's blessing was it that I could still do similar arithmetic? Before we disappear, before we disappear, I mean.

How perfect was that spring day? After finishing work, I dozed off on a station bench and fell into a perfect sleep. Then I opened my eyes. I was thirsty. I drank my usual cup of Mirinda and felt the fizzy rays of the spring sun prickle my skin. The sun's rays, which were naturally No Ice, held that much more warmth within them. *Aah*. I stretched

앉았다. 막상 앉으니—기린은 앉은키가 엄청나고, 전체적으로 다소곳하고 무신경한 느낌이었다. 기린은 이쪽을 쳐다보지도 않는데, 나는 혼자 울고 있었다. 이상하게도 자꾸만 눈물이 나오는 것이었다. 아버지…… 곧장 나는 가슴속의 말을 꺼냈고, 기린의 무릎 위에 내 손을 올려놓았다. 떨리는 손바닥을 통해, 손으로 밀어본 사람만이 기억하는 양복의 질감이 그대로 느껴져 왔다. 구름의 그림자가 빠르게 지나갔다. 기린은 여전히 아무 반응이 없었다. 아버지, 아버지 맞죠?

어떻게 된 거예요? 기린의 무릎을 흔들던 나는, 결국 반응을 포기하고 이런저런 집안의 근황을 들려주었다. 할머니의 소식과 어머니의 회복, 그리고 나는 부동산 일을 배울 수도 있다, 선배가 자꾸 함께 일을 하자고 한다, 자리가, 자리가 있다고 한다. 경제도 차차 좋아질 거라고 한다, 무디스가 어디서 우리의 신용등급이 또 한 계단 올라섰대요, 좋아졌어요. 그러니 돌아오세요. 이제 걱정 안 하셔도 된다니까요. 구름의 그림자가 또 빠르게 지나갔다. 아버지, 그럼 한마디만 해주세요, 네? 아버지 맞죠? 그것만 얘기해줘요.

out my legs and tilted my head back. The clouds were still drifting and the earth was spinning, and when I stretched out my head, I spotted a strange face floating near the platform roof on the other side. No way, it can't be,

a giraffe. It really was a giraffe. The giraffe was smartly dressed in a suit, and it was slowly strolling back and forth along the platform. The station wasn't crowded, but even so, how could no one be paying attention? Everyone was acting like it was no big deal. I kept a close eye on the giraffe, thinking, come on, shouldn't at least one person be alarmed by this? Bobbing its head, the giraffe walked to a bench near the corner and stopped. Then, it SAT. I have to say, "Then, it SAT," because it was such a sweeping, disjointed movement. Oddly enough in that moment, it occurred to me that the giraffe was my dad. I don't know why, but I was sure of it. I was already running through the station. Before he disappears, before he disappears.

To my relief, the giraffe was sitting completely still. I hesitantly made my way over to it, then care-

무관심한, 그러나 잿빛의 눈동자가 이윽고 물끄러미 나를 바라보았다. 기린은 자신의 앞발을 내 손 위에 포개더니, 천천히, 이렇게 얘기했다.

그렇습니까? 기린입니다.

『카스테라』, 문학동네, 2005

fully and hesitantly sat down. Once I was right next to it, I realized how tall the giraffe was, even when it was sitting, and on the whole it seemed gentle and indifferent. The giraffe didn't even look my way, but I was crying to myself. Strangely enough, the tears wouldn't stop coming. Dad... I pulled out the word that was in my heart and placed my hand on the giraffe's knee. Through my trembling palm, I could feel the texture of the suit that only someone who had pushed it before with his hands would remember. The shadow of the clouds zoomed by. The giraffe didn't react. Dad, Dad, it's you, right?

Please tell me what happened. I shook the giraffe's knee, but in the end gave up on getting a response and talked instead about how the family was doing. News about Grandma and Mom's recovery, and how I could learn how to do real estate, and how one of the older guys was trying to get me into the trade, how he said there was an opening. People say the economy is supposed to get better, Moody's or whatever upgraded our credit ratings, so things are getting better. So come home. You don't have to worry anymore. The shadow of the clouds zoomed past again. Dad, just tell me one thing, okay? It's you, right? Just tell me that.

At last, the indifferent, but ash-colored, eyes turned to look at me vacantly. The giraffe lay its hoof over my hand and slowly spoke.

Is that so? I'm a giraffe.

Translated by Sora Kim-Russell

* English translation first published in the *Asia Literary Review*, No. 23.

해설

Afterword

각자도생의 시대

김남혁 (문학평론가)

한국에서 신예 작가의 등장을 두고 제2의 박민규가 출현했다고 과찬하거나 문청들의 습작을 두고 박민규 스타일에서 벗어나지 못했다고 지적하는 장면을 접하는 건 이제 낯선 일이 아니다. 이 같이 모순되는 장면은 2000년대 한국 문학사에서 박민규 소설이 차지하는 자리를 우회적으로 보여준다. 그의 스타일은 1987년 민주화 이후 진행된 한국의 정치·경제·문화적 상황에 응전할 수 있는 활력을 지니기에 충분히 여러 작가들에 의해 모방될 가치가 있지만, 다른 한편 미학적 질감이 너무나 독특해서 따라 하는 순간 아류로 전락하기에 반복해서는 안 되는 자리에 그의 소설이 놓인다.

A Dog-eat-dog World

Kim Nam-hyeok (literary critic)

It is no longer unusual to hear some critic praise a new writer by referring to him or her as "a young Park Min-gyu," or to criticize a young writer as "unable to grow out of the Park Min-gyu narrative." This paradoxical reality hints at the influence of Park's novels in the 21st century Korean literary world. His narrative style has, on the one hand, a perfect dynamic force that can take on the challenges of discussing Korea's political, economic, and cultural issues since its democratization in 1987. This certainly makes it more than worth the trouble for writers who have been trying to emulate his style. On the other hand, the narrative has a very unique aesthetic texture making it so that any

「그렇습니까? 기린입니다」(2004) 역시 박민규 소설의 세계관과 개성이 엮어내는 보편성과 단독성을 잘 보여주는 작품이다. 이 작품의 주인공은 상업고등학교에 다니면서 여러 아르바이트를 전전한다. 이 소설의 중심 사건은 주인공이 출근 시간 신도림역에서 승객들을 만원 지하철 안으로 밀어 넣는 '푸시맨' 일을 하는 도중에 발생한다. 그런데 푸시맨은 박민규가 소설 속에 허구적으로 설정한 소재가 아니라 실제 1990년대 한국 사회에 등장했다가 지금은 사라진 시간제 근무직이다. 1990년 2월 1일부터 서울지하철공사는 출근길 혼잡이 극심한 20개 주요 역에 오전 7시부터 오전 10시까지 아르바이트 대학생 132명을 푸시맨으로 배치해 승객들의 승하차를 돕게 했다. 푸시맨이 활동하던 그해 뉴스를 검색하다 보면 지하철을 이용하려던 시민들이 전동차의 유리를 파손하거나 역장을 구타했다는 기사를 간간이 볼 수 있는데, 그 파손과 구타의 원인은 대부분 지하철의 연착에 있었다. 이런 소동에서 보듯 푸시맨의 등장은 출근 시간을 엄수하려는 시민들의 요구와 관련이 있다. 그런데 흥미롭게도 이와 유사한 일이 한국에 전차가 막 등장했던 시대에도 일어난 적이 있다. 서대문에서 청량

writer attempting to mimic him can produce no more than a cheap imitation.

"Is That So? I'm A Giraffe" (2004) is a good example of Park's worldview and quirk blending together to create both accessibility and uniqueness. The protagonist of this story goes to a vocational high school and works one temp job after another. The main incident of the story happens during one of his temp jobs as the "pushman" whose job is to push passengers into packed train cars at Sindorim Station. This "pushman" is, in fact, not a fictional occupation that Park dreamt up, but a real temporary position that existed in Korea in the 1990s and has since disappeared. Starting from February 1st, 1990, the Seoul Metro hired 132 college-aged workers to help passengers board the subway cars at the twenty stations with the most traffic during rush hour from 7 to 10a.m. Several news articles related to "pushmen" from the 1990s report incidents in which citizens broke the train car windows or assaulted the stationmaster, usually out of frustration related to train delays. As these incidents indicate, passengers who wanted to get to work on time enabled the creation of "pushmen." Interestingly, a similar incident occurred when the street-

리를 잇는 팔 킬로미터의 선로 위로 노상 전차가 조선에 처음 모습을 드러내고 고작 열흘이 지난 광무 3년(1899년) 5월 26일에 시민들은 전차를 소각하고 전차장을 구타했다. 포전병문(布廛屛門, 지금의 종로 2가) 앞을 지나던 전차가 다섯 살 어린이를 치어 죽이자 이를 지켜보던 군중들은 전차에 돌을 던지고 불을 질렀다. '전차 소각 사건'으로 기록된 이 사건을 계기로 전차 회사는 차량마다 큰 경종을 달았고 시민들의 안전을 중시했다. 그런데 대략 백 년의 시간차를 두고 대중교통을 상대로 발생한 두 사건은 겉으로 보기에 유사하지만 사실상 전혀 다른 원인과 결과를 함축하고 있다. 개화기 조선인에게 전차는 문명개화의 목표로 일로매진케 하는 선망의 대상이었지만, 다른 한편 자신들의 고유한 삶의 터전을 파괴할지 모르는 공포의 대상이기도 했다. 선망과 공포가 만들어내는 정신적 긴장이 전차 소각 사건으로 이어졌다면, 1990년대 시민들이 대중교통을 상대로 일으킨 사건들은 지배 체제에 대한 온전한 투항에서 비롯됐다. 그래서 전차를 향한 조선인들의 공격은 전차 회사로 대변되는 신문명의 작동 메커니즘을 미약하나마 교정하도록 하는 결과를 이끌어냈지만, 서울 시민들의

car first appeared in Korea. On May 26 1899, a mere ten days after the streetcar that traveled on an 8-kilometer track between Seodaemun and Cheongnyangni started running, citizens set a streetcar on fire and assaulted the streetcar conductor. When the streetcar ran over and killed a five-year-old child in front of the Pojeonbyeongmun station (present day Jongno-2-ga), the bystanders threw stones at the streetcar and set it on fire. After this incident, recorded in history books as the "Streetcar Burning Incident," the streetcar company added horns to all streetcars and took new safety precautions. These two incidents related to public transportation, which happened approximately a century apart, appear to be similar but in fact have completely different motivations and implications. To the Joseon people at the beginning of modernization, the streetcar was an object of desire that embodied the drive for modernization, but also an object of fear that posed a threat to their unique way of life. While the streetcar incident was the result of the tension between desire and fear, the subways incidents of the 1990s were simply capitulations to the ruling system. Thus, the streetcar incident results in an adjustment—albeit a very

공격은 역설적이게도 시민들 스스로 지배 체제에 자발적으로 복종하도록 하는 결과를 낳았다. 그렇기에 푸시맨은 시민들의 자발적 복종을 돕는 인물, 다시 말해 이들이 낙오되지 않도록 지배 체제 속으로 밀어 넣는 사람이다. 백 년의 시간 동안 도대체 한국에서 무슨 일이 일어났기에 시민들이 이렇게 변한 것일까? 푸시맨까지 등장한 이유가 무엇인가? 이러한 질문에 대해 「그렇습니까? 기린입니다」는 이렇게 답하고 있다. "승객 여러분들은 안전선 밖으로 물러나 주셔야겠지만, 그게 될 리가 없는 것이다. 승객들은 모두 전철을 타야 하고, 전철엔 이미 탈 자리가 없다. 타지 않으면, 늦는다. 신체의 안전선은 이곳이지만, 삶의 안전선은 전철 속이다. 당신이라면, 어느 곳을 택하겠는가?"

그렇다. 이제 1899년의 '전차 소각 사건'이 보여주듯 신체의 안전선과 삶의 안전선이 팽팽히 경합하던 시대는 지났다. 지금은 신체의 안전선을 전철(지배 체제)이 제공하는 삶의 안전선과 일치시켜야만 하는 시대이다. 그럴 수 없다면 신체의 안전선을 포기해서라도 삶의 안전선으로 투항해야 한다. 어째서 그러한가. 한국은 1987년 6월 혁명으로 군사독재정부를 무너뜨리고 민주

small one—to new technology represented by the streetcar, but the subways incidents paradoxically resulted in the Seoul citizens' voluntary subjugation to the establishment. Therefore, the role of the "pushmen" was to aid the citizen's voluntary surrender, to push them into the establishment so that no one would fall behind. What changed Koreans in the hundred years after 1899? How did Koreans come to need "pushmen?" "Is That So? I'm A Giraffe" answers, "Everyone has to get on the train, but there's no more room. If you don't get on, you'll be late. The body's safety line may be here, but life's yellow line is inside the train. Which one would you choose?"

In 1899 the tension between physical safety and survival pushed and pulled each other back and forth, but that is no longer the case today. These days, the physical safety line must be superimposed on the train's survival line (establishment). If the two are still distinct, then one must give up on physical safety to charge toward the survival line. Why is this so? The revolution of June 1987 overthrew the military *junta* in Korea and finally achieved democracy, but more problems were left for many citizens to solve in the intersection be-

주의를 실현했으나 대다수 시민들에게 문제는 여전히 남아 있었다. 그 문제는 자유화와 민주화라는 프로젝트의 교착상태에서 비롯됐다. 더불어 영국의 대처와 미국의 레이건 정부에서 시작된 신자유주의 정책의 확산과 공산권 국가들의 붕괴는 민주화 이후 한국의 경제적 상황을 보수화시키는 데 일조했다. 평등하고 자유로운 공동체를 꿈꾸던 민주주의는 형식적으로나마 실현됐으나 실제로 모든 국민은 각자도생해야 하는 시대가 펼쳐진 것이다. 독재를 물리치고 되찾은 자유는 시장만능주의 안에 국한된 자유로 축소됐다. 「그렇습니까? 기린입니다」는 이러한 시대적 변화를 배경으로 삼고 있다. 이 소설에서 푸시맨인 주인공은 자신의 '삶의 안전선'을 지키기 위해서 타인의 '신체의 안전선'을 무시할 수밖에 없고, 그렇기에 "저 사람들을 사람이라고 생각하지" 않은 채 "화물"로 간주해야만 간신히 살아남는 시대에 놓여 있다. 그런데 문제는 짐짝 취급해야 하는 대상에 어느 누구도 예외가 될 수 없다는 점이다. 주인공 자신이 살아남기 위해 아버지마저도 지하철 속으로 밀어 넣어야 하는 비극이 아무렇지도 않게 자행된다. 1990년대 실제로 일어났던 역장 구타 사건에서 보듯 지배 체제가

tween liberalization and democratization. The spread of the neo-liberalist policies that began with Thatcher and Reagan, and the fall of the communist states contributed to the conservative shift of the Korean economy since democratization. Democracy and its dreams of equality and freedom did come true, if only on the surface. Economically, it was now every man for himself. The freedom earned by bringing an end to tyranny turned out to be freedom within the confining laws of an unbridled free market economy. "Is That So? I'm A Giraffe" is set in this period. The protagonist cannot help but ignore the passengers' physical safety line in order to protect his own survival line, and therefore should not think of the passengers as people, but rather as cargo in order to survive. Unfortunately, there is no exception to this rule, and the protagonist ends up pushing his own father into the subway car. This tragic reality is not even seen as tragic. As we can witness in the 1990s subway incidents, the citizens' fierce dedication to live by the rules of the establishment comes from this historical context—one in which it was every man for himself, even if it meant treating others like cargo to protect one's own survival.

만들어 놓은 질서를 엄수하려는 시민들의 자발적 복종은 바로 이 같은 맥락에서 비롯됐다. 자신의 삶의 안전선을 지키기 위해 타인을 무감히 짐짝 취급하며 각자도생해야 하는 시대적 맥락 말이다.

「그렇습니까? 기린입니다」에서 아버지는 끝내 이 같은 시대적 맥락에서 일탈한다. 시간이 흘러 지하철을 타지 않고 사라진 아버지는 기린이 되어 돌아온다. 이는 흡사 카프카의 저 유명한 「변신」을 연상케 하는 장면일 텐데, 그 누구도 아버지의 변신을 두려워한다거나 알아보지 않는다는 점에서 카프카의 작품보다 끔찍한 비극성을 드러낸다. 세상의 질서에서 낙오된 사람은 플랫폼 위의 기린처럼 이질적인 존재지만 그렇다고 어느 누구의 관심도 받을 수 없는 이른바 '인간쓰레기'이기 때문이다. 각자도생의 삶에서 낙오된 아버지는 어느 누구와도 소통할 수 없고, 어느 누구에게도 인식의 경종을 울릴 수 없는 비인간이 되어 버린다. 이렇듯 박민규의 소설은 유쾌한 화법과 독특한 상상력으로 한국 사회의 무겁고도 비극적인 문제들을 날카롭게 포착하기에, 그의 소설을 읽는 독자들은 한바탕 웃고 난 후 밀려드는 씁쓸함을 곱씹게 된다. 이제 이 글을 마감하는 자리

In "Is That So? I'm A Giraffe," the protagonist's father derails from this historical context in the end. Time passes, and the father who did not get on the subway returns as a giraffe. This scene echoes Kafka's roach, but illustrates a much deeper tragedy in that no one is aware of this transformation, let alone appalled. Falling behind the times is a taboo that turns a person into something as bizarre as a giraffe on a subway platform, and as unworthy of attention as garbage. Left behind in the dog-eat-dog world, the father becomes a non-human who cannot communicate with anyone or be a warning to the rest of society. Park's lighthearted narrative and distinctive imagination thus captures a brutally honest view of the sobering, tragic realities of Korean society that Park's readers cannot help but to experience a bitter aftertaste that follows the laughter. We have one last question remaining at the end of this commentary: How do we cope in a dog-eat-dog society that turns losers into giraffes? How do we recover the sound judgment demonstrated by the Joseon people in the 1899 streetcar incident? The answers to these questions are why we must go on reading Park Min-gyu.

에서 우리에게 남은 마지막 질문이 있다. 그렇다면 체제의 낙오자를 기린으로 변신시키는 각자도생의 시대에 우리는 어떻게 응전할 수 있는가. 1899년 '전차 소각 사건'을 일으킨 조선인들이 보여준 정신적 긴장을 우리는 어떻게 되찾을 수가 있을까. 우리가 계속해서 박민규의 소설을 따라 읽어야 하는 이유가 이 질문에 담겨 있다.

비평의 목소리
Critical Acclaim

박민규 소설은 요약하기가 참 어렵다. 사실적인 이야기든 또는 우화적인 이야기든 이야기 위주의 구성이 아니기 때문이다. 사실 박민규의 소설은 중간에 덮었다가 다시 읽으려고 하면 힘이 든다. 처음부터 다시 읽어야 한다. 이것은 시의 특성과 통한다. 그의 장편『삼미 슈퍼스타즈의 마지막 팬클럽』에도 이런 기법이 살아 있다. 『카스테라』를 읽으면서 훌륭한 작가임을 재확인했고 내 나름으로 '한국 문학의 보람'을 느꼈다.

백낙청

『지구영웅전설』은 문학의 어떤 의자에도 편히 앉지

Park Min-gyu's stories are very difficult to summarize. Whether it is realistic or allegorical, his stories are not structured around the plot. Park's stories are difficult to leave and return to. One must start again from the beginning. In this respect, his stories are similar to poetry. This technique is palpable in *The Last Fan Club Of The Sammi Superstars*. He was confirmed a great writer through *Castella*, and he has reaffirmed my faith in Korean literature.

Baek Nak-cheong

The Legend Of Earth Heroes does not fit snugly into any literary category. It reads like a fantasy but feels more like satire, but then it feels more like

않는다. 판타지인가 싶으면 판타지의 의자에서 풍자로 가고, 풍자인가 싶으면 풍자의 의자에서 냉소로 간다. 냉소인가 하면 냉소의 건너편에 가서 블랙코미디가 된다. 그 블랙코미디는 또 그리 코미디가 아니다. 그러므로 내가 보기에 이 작가의 재능은 탁월한 미끄러지기에 있는 듯하다.

도정일

그 모든 것을 포함하여 박민규의 소설은 2000년대 후기 자본주의 시대 한국 소설의 변화를 보여주는 중요한 징표이다. 그중 하나는 이 시대 한국 소설이 새로운 형태의 개인주의를 창안하고 있다는 것과 관련 있다. 박민규 소설의 인물들은 자본주의적 삶의 양태 속에서 부유하는 주변부적·소시민적 삶의 고통을 안고 있으면서도 그 고통에 지나치게 집착하거나 매몰되지도 않고, 그렇다고 적극 저항하지도 않는다. 대신 그들이 취하는 선택은 그 고통을 분산시키기 위해 현실과는 동떨어진 비일상적인 대상에 리비도를 비끄러매 투사하면서 지금 이 현실이 아닌 다른 곳으로 시선을 돌리는 것이다. 박민규의 소설에서 부유하는 키치적 대중문화 기표와

cynicism than satire. Upon closer examination, however, the story transcends cynicism and turns into black comedy, but there is nothing funny about this black comedy. I think this writer's talent is his unparalleled ability to elude categorization.

Do Jeong-il

Park Min-gyu's stories are an important indicator of the changes Korean literature underwent in the post-capitalist Korean society of the 21st century. One of these indicators is closely related to Korean literature's creation of a new form of individualism. The characters in Park's novels float aimlessly through life, carrying around with them the pain of being on the periphery of society, but they are not consumed by their pain, nor do they try to resist the system that causes pain. What they do instead is project their libidos onto objects that are far removed from reality so as to distract from the pain and keep their attention elsewhere. The kitschy signifiers of popular culture and play on words, the hallmarks of Park's writing, are light, effective tools for expressing these attitudes and redirecting attention. This strategy is a way of remembering and preserving the better, self-fulfilled person inside

말의 향유는 그런 그들의 태도를 투사해 실어 나르는 가볍고 효과적인 표정 분산의 도구라 할 수 있다. 그것은 한편으로 일상의 왜소한 자아와는 다른 자리에 있는 자기충일적인 자아를 기억하고 보존하면서 현실의 고통을 에둘러 유희적으로 표면을 미끄러져가는 개인 전략이다.

김영찬

지금껏 발표된 그의 소설에서는 항상 유머와 비장감, 골계와 숭고라는 기묘한 복식조가 박진감 넘치는 랠리를 벌인다. 그 게임은 과연 쿨하고 도발적이지만, 차갑거나 건조하지는 않다. 자신을 포함한 인간 일반을 가엾게 여기는 마음과 낙원을 그리는 상상이 간절히 거듭되는 박민규 소설의 속살은 뜨겁고 보드랍다.

김혜리

박민규에게서 뭔가를 빼앗아올 수 있다면 나는 주저하지 않고, 그가 창안하여 우리에게 덥석 안겨준, 그 놀랍고도 새로운 문장을 가져올 것이다. 그는 지금껏 우리 문학계에 존재한 적 없었던 기이하고 유쾌한 문장들

the insignificant existence of everyday life, and deflecting the pain within by gliding across on the surface of humor.

Kim Yeong-chan

In every one of Park Min-gyu's stories published to date, there has always been a gripping doubles' rally between humor and sobriety, and satire and sublimity. The games are always detached and provocative, but not cold or dry. The earnest recurrence of Park's sympathy for humanity—including himself—and the imagination that yearns for paradise makes up the warm, soft underbelly of Park's stories.

Kim Hye-ri

If I could steal one thing from Park Min-gyu, I would, without giving it another thought, go for the new, amazing sentences he created and presented to us. He has written peculiar, delightful sentences that have never existed before in Korean literature, and prompted the sweet surrender of readers and fellow writers alike. Colloquial and literary at the same time, his narrative of pity is disguised as a narrative of humor, which he utilizes craftily to

을 제시하여 나를 비롯한 프로페셔널과 독자들의 유쾌한 항복 선언을 받아내고 있다. 구어이면서 동시에 문어인 그의 문장들은 유희적 태도로 가장한 연민의 어법을 능청스럽게 구사하며 우리를 행복한 독서의 경험으로 끌어들인다. '新언문일치체'라 불러도 좋을 그의 문장들이 오래 기다려온 비처럼 내 온몸을 두들기기 시작하면 나는 나의 어두운 골방 속에서 남몰래 책으로 얼굴을 가리고 조용히 웃는다.

김영하

bring us a fulfilling reading experience. When his sentences, which may be referred to as "new colloquial-literary style," come down on me like rain upon parched land, I sit in a dark room, cover my face with the book, and smile noiselessly.

Kim Young-ha

번역 **김소라** Translated by Sora Kim-Russell

김소라는 이화여자대학교에서 강의를 하고 있다. 신경숙의 『어디선가 나를 찾는 전화벨이 울리고』(2014)와 공지영의 『우리들의 행복한 시간』(2014)을 번역한 바 있으며, 다른 번역 작품들은 『미국 독자, 아시아 문학 리뷰』『진달래: 한국 문학과 문화 잡지』 외 다른 출판물에서 발표되고 있다.

Sora Kim-Russell teaches at Ewha Womans University in Seoul. She has translated Shin Kyung-sook's *I'll Be Right There* and Gong Ji-young's *Our Happy Time* (both forthcoming April 2014), and her other work has appeared in *The American Reader*, *Asia Literary Review*, *Azalea: Journal of Korean Literature & Culture*, and other publications.

감수 **전승희** Edited by Jeon Seung-hee

전승희는 서울대학교와 하버드대학교에서 영문학과 비교문학으로 박사 학위를 받았으며, 현재 하버드대학교 한국학 연구소의 연구원으로 재직하며 아시아 문예 계간지 《ASIA》 편집위원으로 활동 중이다. 현대 한국문학 및 세계문학을 다룬 논문을 다수 발표했으며, 바흐친의 『장편소설과 민중언어』, 제인 오스틴의 『오만과 편견』 등을 공역했다. 1988년 한국여성연구소의 창립과 《여성과 사회》의 창간에 참여했고, 2002년부터 보스턴 지역 피학대 여성을 위한 단체인 '트랜지션하우스' 운영에 참여해 왔다. 2006년 하버드대학교 한국학 연구소에서 '한국 현대사와 기억'을 주제로 한 워크숍을 주관했다.

Jeon Seung-hee is a member of the Editorial Board of *ASIA*, and a Fellow at the Korea Institute, Harvard University. She received a Ph.D. in English Literature from Seoul National University and a Ph.D. in Comparative Literature from Harvard University. She has presented and published numerous papers on modern Korean and world literature. She is also a co-translator of Mikhail Bakhtin's *Novel and the People's Culture* and Jane Austen's *Pride and Prejudice*. She is a founding member of the Korean Women's Studies Institute and of the biannual Women's Studies' journal *Women and Society* (1988), and she has been working at 'Transition House,' the first and oldest shelter for battered women in New England. She organized a workshop entitled "The Politics of Memory in Modern Korea" at the Korea Institute, Harvard University, in 2006. She also served as an advising committee member for the Asia-Africa Literature Festival in 2007 and for the POSCO Asian Literature Forum in 2008.

바이링궐 에디션 한국 대표 소설 034
그렇습니까? 기린입니다

2013년 10월 25일 초판 1쇄 발행
2023년 6월 15일 초판 6쇄 발행

지은이 박민규 | **옮긴이** 김소라 | **펴낸이** 김재범
감수 전승희 | **기획** 정은경, 전성태, 이경재
디자인 나루기획 | **인쇄·제책** 굿에그커뮤니케이션 | **종이** 한솔PNS
펴낸곳 아시아 | **출판등록** 2006년 1월 27일 제406-2006-000004호
주소 경기도 파주시 회동길 445
전화 031.944.5058 | **팩스** 070.7611.2505 | **전자우편** bookasia@hanmail.net
ISBN 978-89-94006-94-9 (set) | 978-89-94006-98-7 (04810)
값은 뒤표지에 있습니다.

Bi-lingual Edition Modern Korean Literature 034
Is That So? I'm A Giraffe

Written by Park Min-gyu | **Translated by** Sora Kim-Russell
Published by ASIA Publishers
Address 445, Hoedong-gil, Paju-si, Gyeonggi-do, Korea
Tel. (8231).944.5058 | **E-mail** bookasia@hanmail.net
First published in Korea by Asia Publishers 2013
ISBN 978-89-94006-94-9(set) | 978-89-94006-98-7(04810)

바이링궐 에디션 한국 대표 소설 목록

001 **병신과 머저리** 이청준 / 제니퍼 리
002 **어둠의 혼** 김원일 / 손석주, 캐서린 로즈 토레스
003 **순이삼촌** 현기영 / 이정희
004 **엄마의 말뚝 1** 박완서 / 유영난
005 **유형의 땅** 조정래 / 전경자
006 **무진기행** 김승옥 / 케빈 오록
007 **삼포 가는 길** 황석영/ 김우창
008 **아홉 켤레의 구두로 남은 사내** 윤흥길 / 브루스 풀턴, 주찬 풀턴
009 **돌아온 우리의 친구** 신상웅 / 손석주, 캐서린 로즈 토레스
010 **원미동 시인** 양귀자 / 전미세리
011 **중국인 거리** 오정희 / 주찬 풀턴, 브루스 풀턴
012 **풍금이 있던 자리** 신경숙 / 아그니타 테넌트
013 **하나코는 없다** 최윤 / 주찬 풀턴, 브루스 풀턴
014 **인간에 대한 예의** 공지영 / 주찬 풀턴, 브루스 풀턴
015 **빈처** 은희경 / 전승희
016 **필론의 돼지** 이문열 / 제이미 챙
017 **슬로우 불릿** 이대환 / 전승희
018 **직선과 독가스** 임철우 / 크리스 최
019 **깃발** 홍희담 / 전승희
020 **새벽 출정** 방현석 / 주다희, 안선재
021 **별을 사랑하는 마음으로** 윤후명 / 전미세리
022 **목련공원** 이승우 / 유진 라르센-할록
023 **칼에 찔린 자국** 김인숙 / 손석주, 캐서린 로즈 토레스
024 **회복하는 인간** 한강 / 전승희
025 **트렁크** 정이현 / 브루스 풀턴, 주찬 풀턴
026 **판문점** 이호철 / 테오도르 휴즈
027 **수난 이대** 하근찬 / 케빈 오록
055 **봄밤** 권여선 / 전승희

028 **분지** 남정현 / 전승희
029 **봄 실상사** 정도상 / 전승희
030 **은행나무 사랑** 김하기 / 손석주, 캐서린 로즈 토레스
031 **눈사람 속의 검은 항아리** 김소진 / 크리스 최
032 **오후, 가로지르다** 하성란 / 전승희
033 **나는 봉천동에 산다** 조경란 / 쉥크 카리
034 **그렇습니까? 기린입니다** 박민규 / 김소라
035 **성탄특선** 김애란 / 제이미 챙
036 **무자년의 가을 사흘** 서정인 / 제이미 챙
037 **유자소전** 이문구 / 제이미 챙
038 **향기로운 우물 이야기** 박범신 / 마야 웨스트
039 **월행** 송기원 / 제인 리
040 **협죽도 그늘 아래** 성석제 / 전승희
041 **아겔다마** 박상륭 / 전승희
042 **내 영혼의 우물** 최인석 / 전승희
043 **당신에 대해서** 이인성 / 마야 웨스트
044 **회색 시** 배수아 / 장정화, 앤드류 제임스 키스트
045 **브라운 부인** 정영문 / 정영문
046 **속옷** 김남일 / 전승희
047 **상하이에 두고 온 사람들** 공선옥 / 전승희
048 **모두에게 복된 새해** 김연수 / 마야 웨스트
049 **코끼리** 김재영 / 미셸 주은 김
050 **먼지별** 이경 / 전미세리
051 **혜자의 눈꽃** 천승세 / 전승희
052 **아베의 가족** 전상국 / 손석주
053 **문 앞에서** 이동화 / 전미세리
054 **그리고, 축제** 이혜경 / 브루스 풀턴, 주찬 풀턴
083 **상춘곡** 윤대녕 / 테레사 김

056 **오늘의 운세** 한창훈 / 케롱 린
057 **새** 전성태 / 전승희
058 **밀수록 다시 가까워지는** 이기호 / 테레사 김
059 **유리방패** 김중혁 / 케빈 오록
060 **전당포를 찾아서** 김종광 / 손석주
061 **도둑견습** 김주영 / 손석주
062 **사랑하라, 희망 없이** 윤영수 / 전승희
063 **봄날 오후, 과부 셋** 정지아 / 브랜든 맥케일, 김윤경
064 **유턴 지점에 보물지도를 묻다** 윤성희 / 이지은
065 **쁘이거나 쯔이거나** 백가흠 / 장정화, 앤드류 제임스 키스트
066 **나는 음식이다** 오수연 / 크리스 최
067 **트럭** 강영숙 / 전승희
068 **통조림 공장** 편혜영 / 미셸 주은 김
069 **꽃** 부희령 / 리처드 해리스, 김현경
070 **피의일요일** 윤이형 / 전승희
071 **북소리** 송영 / 손석주
072 **발칸의 장미를 내게 주었네** 정미경 / 스텔라 김
073 **아무도 돌아오지 않는 밤** 김숨 / 전미세리
074 **젓가락여자** 천운영 / 전미세리
075 **아직 일어나지 않은 일** 김미월 / 전미세리
076 **언니를 놓치다** 이경자 / 장정화, 앤드류 키스트
077 **아들** 윤정모 / 쉥크 카리
078 **명두** 구효서 / 미셸 주은 김
079 **모독** 조세희 / 손석주
080 **화요일의 강** 손홍규 / 제이미 챙
081 **고수** 이외수 / 손석주
082 **말을 찾아서** 이순원 / 미셸 주은 김
084 **삭매와 자미** 김별아 / 전미세리
085 **저만치 혼자서** 김훈 / 크리스 최
086 **감자** 김동인 / 케빈 오록
087 **운수 좋은 날** 현진건 / 케빈 오록
088 **탈출기** 최서해 / 박선영
089 **과도기** 한설야 / 전승희
090 **지하촌** 강경애 / 서지문
091 **날개** 이상 / 케빈 오록
092 **김 강사와 T 교수** 유진오 / 손석주
093 **소설가 구보씨의 일일** 박태원 / 박선영
094 **비 오는 길** 최명익 / 자넷 풀
095 **빛 속에** 김사량 / 크리스토퍼 스캇
096 **봄 · 봄** 김유정 / 전승희
097 **벙어리 삼룡이** 나도향 / 박선영
098 **달밤** 이태준 / 김종운, 브루스 풀턴
099 **사랑손님과 어머니** 주요섭 / 김종운, 브루스 풀턴
100 **갯마을** 오영수 / 마샬 필
101 **소망** 채만식 / 브루스 풀턴, 주찬 풀턴
102 **두 파산** 염상섭 / 손석주
103 **풀잎** 이효석 / 브루스 풀턴, 주찬 풀턴
104 **맥** 김남천 / 박선영
105 **꺼삐딴 리** 전광용 / 마샬 필
106 **소나기** 황순원 / 에드워드 포이트라스
107 **등신불** 김동리 / 설순봉
108 **요한 시집** 장용학 / 케빈 오록
109 **비 오는 날** 손창섭 / 전승희
110 **오발탄** 이범선 / 마샬 필

K-픽션 시리즈 | Korean Fiction Series

〈K-픽션〉 시리즈는 한국문학의 젊은 상상력입니다. 최근 발표된 가장 우수하고 흥미로운 작품을 엄선하여 출간하는 〈K-픽션〉은 한국문학의 생생한 현장을 국내외 독자들과 실시간으로 공유하고자 기획되었습니다. 〈바이링궐 에디션 한국 대표 소설〉 시리즈를 통해 검증된 탁월한 번역진이 참여하여 원작의 재미와 품격을 최대한 살린 〈K-픽션〉 시리즈는 매 계절마다 새로운 작품을 선보입니다.

001 버핏과의 저녁 식사-**박민규** Dinner with Buffett-**Park Min-gyu**

002 아르판-**박형서** Arpan-**Park hyoung su**

003 애드벌룬-**손보미** Hot Air Balloon-**Son Bo-mi**

004 나의 클린트 이스트우드-**오한기** My Clint Eastwood-**Oh Han-ki**

005 이베리아의 전갈-**최민우** Dishonored-**Choi Min-woo**

006 양의 미래-**황정은** Kong's Garden-**Hwang Jung-eun**

007 대니-**윤이형** Danny-**Yun I-hyeong**

008 퇴근-**천명관** Homecoming-**Cheon Myeong-kwan**

009 옥화-**금희** Ok-hwa-**Geum Hee**

010 시차-**백수린** Time Difference-**Baik Sou linne**

011 올드 맨 리버-**이장욱** Old Man River-**Lee Jang-wook**

012 권순찬과 착한 사람들-**이기호** Kwon Sun-chan and Nice People-**Lee Ki-ho**

013 알바생 자르기-**장강명** Fired-**Chang Kang-myoung**

014 어디로 가고 싶으신가요-**김애란** Where Would You Like To Go?-**Kim Ae-ran**

015 세상에서 가장 비싼 소설-**김민정** The World's Most Expensive Novel-**Kim Min-jung**

016 체스의 모든 것-**김금희** Everything About Chess-**Kim Keum-hee**

017 할로윈-**정한아** Halloween-**Chung Han-ah**

018 그 여름-**최은영** The Summer-**Choi Eunyoung**

019 어느 피씨주의자의 종생기-**구병모** The Story of P.C.-**Gu Byeong-mo**

020 모르는 영역-**권여선** An Unknown Realm-**Kwon Yeo-sun**

021 4월의 눈-**손원평** April Snow-**Sohn Won-pyung**

022 서우-**강화길** Seo-u-**Kang Hwa-gil**

023 가출-**조남주** Run Away-**Cho Nam-joo**

024 연애의 감정학-**백영옥** How to Break Up Like a Winner-**Baek Young-ok**

025 창모-**우다영** Chang-mo-**Woo Da-young**

026 검은 방-**정지아** The Black Room-**Jeong Ji-a**

027 도쿄의 마야-**장류진** Maya in Tokyo-**Jang Ryu-jin**

028 홀리데이 홈-**편혜영** Holiday Home-**Pyun Hye-young**

029 해피 투게더-**서장원** Happy Together-**Seo Jang-won**

030 골드러시-**서수진** Gold Rush-**Seo Su-jin**

031 당신이 보고 싶어하는 세상-**장강명** The World You Want to See-**Chang Kang-myoung**

032 지난밤 내 꿈에-**정한아** Last Night, In My Dream-**Chung Han-ah**

Special 휴가중인 시체-**김중혁** Corpse on Vacation-**Kim Jung-hyuk**

Special 사파에서-**방현석** Love in Sa Pa-**Bang Hyeon-seok**

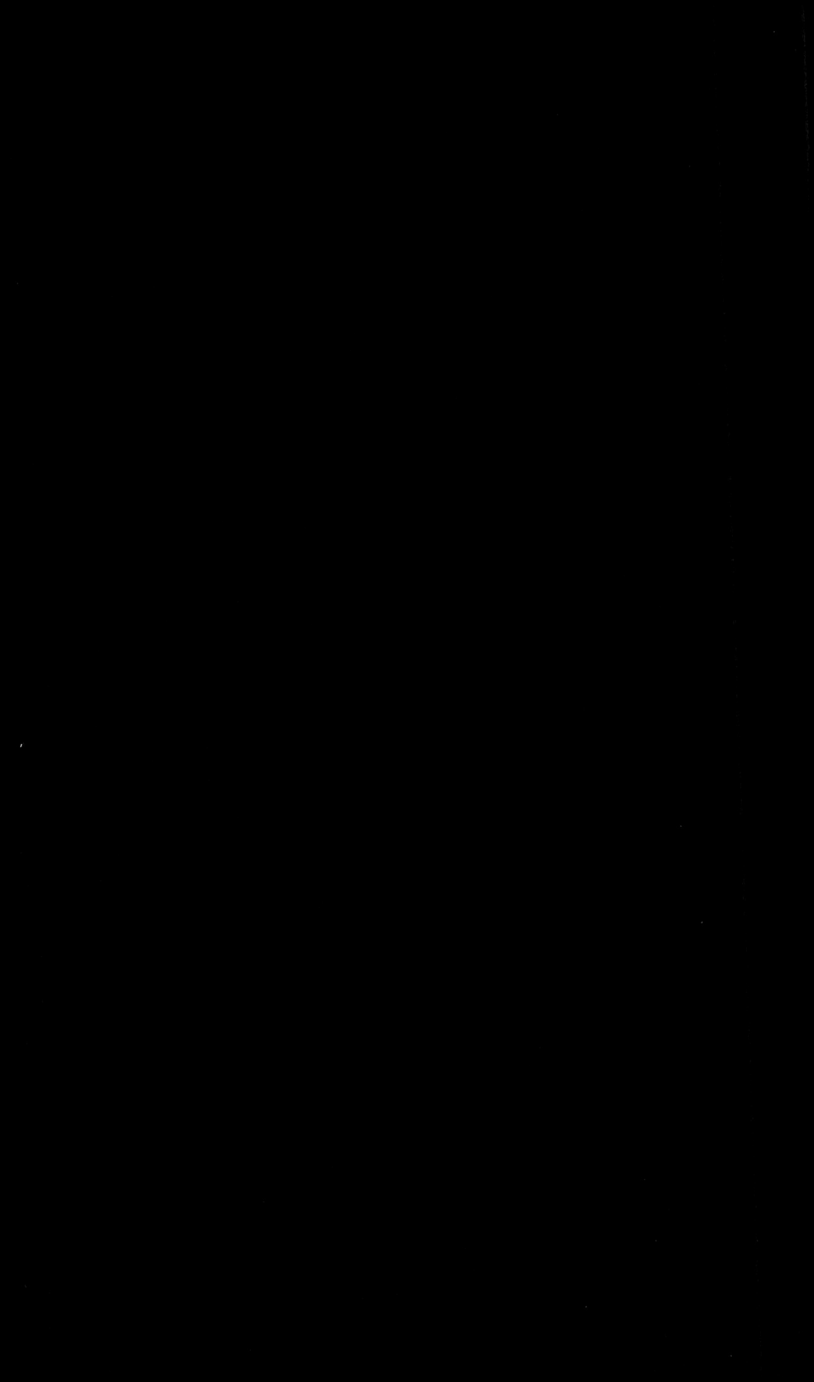